Starscape Books by David Lubar

NOVELS

Flip
Hidden Talents
True Talents

SERIES

My Rotten Life: Nathan Abercrombie, Accidental Zombie, Book One
Dead Guy Spy: Nathan Abercrombie, Accidental Zombie, Book Two
Goop Soup: Nathan Abercrombie, Accidental Zombie, Book Three
The Big Stink: Nathan Abercrombie, Accidental Zombie, Book Four

STORY COLLECTIONS

The Battle of the Red Hot Pepper Weenies
and Other Warped and Creepy Tales

The Curse of the Campfire Weenies
and Other Warped and Creepy Tales

In the Land of the Lawn Weenies
and Other Warped and Creepy Tales

Invasion of the Road Weenies
and Other Warped and Creepy Tales

Nathan Abercrombie,
Accidental Zombie

BOOK FIVE

ENTER THE ZOMBIE

David Lubar

STARSCAPE

DISCARD

A Tom Doherty Associates Book · New York

MOORESVILLE PUBLIC LIBRARY
220 WEST HARRISON STREET
MOORESVILLE, INDIANA 46158

This is a work of fiction. All of the characters, organizations, and events portrayed in this novel are either products of the author's imagination or are used fictitiously.

ENTER THE ZOMBIE

Copyright © 2010 by David Lubar

Reader's Guide copyright © 2010 by Tor Books

All rights reserved.

A Starscape Book
Published by Tom Doherty Associates, LLC
175 Fifth Avenue
New York, NY 10010

www.tor-forge.com

Library of Congress Cataloging-in-Publication Data

Lubar, David.
    Enter the zombie / David Lubar. — 1st ed.
        p. cm.
    "A Tor book"—Verso t.p.
    Summary: When the head of the Bureau of Useful Misadventures (or
BUM) discovers that an evil organization is using the Student Mind and Body
competition to recruit agents, he asks Nathan to enter the competition, but
things go terribly wrong when Nathan's nemesis starts to notice some odd
things about him, and Nathan fears his zombie identity will be exposed.
    ISBN 978-0-7653-2672-0 (trade paperback.)
    ISBN 978-0-7653-2344-6 (hardcover)
    [1. Zombies—Fiction.   2. Schools—Fiction.   3. Spies—Fiction.]   I. Title.
    PZ7.L96775En 2011
    [Fic]—dc22

                                                                    2010036110

First Edition: January 2011

Printed in December 2010 in the United States of America by RR Donnelley,
Harrisonburg, Virginia

0 9 8 7 6 5 4 3 2 1

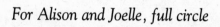

For Alison and Joelle, full circle

CONTENTS

INTRODUCTION

Winter is over. I used to like spring. But when you're dead, and trying not to rot too fast, the last thing you look forward to is warm air and sunshine.

1

Mission Irresistible

"That can't be him." I froze at the bottom of the school steps and stared at the man on the sidewalk twenty yards ahead of me. It was a Monday afternoon in early March, and we'd just gotten out of school.

"Which means it has to be him," Mookie said. "He's really tricky, right? So I'll bet he's disguised to look like himself, just to throw people off."

"It's definitely him," Abigail said when we were ten yards away. "There can't possibly be two tall, thin red-headed men on earth with ears that large."

"Wait!" Mookie grabbed my arm. "It could be one of his robots. We should wait here until it explodes."

11

"It's not a robot," I said. "They do a good job with the squirrels, but the human ones never look that real. It's him. I still can't believe this."

I thought nothing Mr. Murphy did would surprise me. As the head of BUM—the Bureau of Useful Misadventures—he'd tossed me to a pack of vicious guard dogs, sent me over an electrified fence, made me think I was about to get blown up, and nearly burned down my house. He even had me claw my way through a mountain of garbage. At least he hadn't made me chew my way through the trash heaps with my hands tied behind my back.

After my adventure on the garbage barge, I'd spent several months carrying out other spy missions for BUM. I'd saved a lot of lives, and helped the good guys catch some really evil bad guys.

During that time, Mr. Murphy contacted me in dozens of strange and dangerous ways involving all sorts of mechanical creatures, lots of sparks, a scattering of laser beams, far too many flames, and a variety of explosions.

But there was one thing he'd never done after I'd joined BUM.

Until today.

"This must be serious," I said.

"It's definitely unprecedented," Abigail said.

"He's not a president," Mookie said. "At least, I

don't think he is. And if he was, he probably wouldn't tell anyone."

Abigail groaned, but didn't bother to say anything. I had a feeling I knew what *unprecedented* meant. This had never happened before, not counting the first time Mr. Murphy had approached me. But it was happening now. The master spy who had recruited me and trained me, the man who did everything in secret, was standing in public, right in front of the school, waiting for me. He wasn't even wearing any sort of disguise or hiding behind a large plant.

"We need to talk," he said when I reached him.

I couldn't even begin to guess what this was about.

"We'll catch up with you," Abigail said. She tugged at Mookie's arm. "Come on. Let's leave them alone."

"Hold on. We *all* need to talk." Mr. Murphy tucked his little finger under his thumb, then aimed his other fingers in our direction. "The three of you. Right now. But let's not stand here where we'll attract attention."

He headed down the street. I stared at his back for a moment, then raced to catch up with him.

"Well, that certainly won't attract any attention," he said. "Would you like to hop and skip, too? Or is running enough? You could sing at the top of your lungs. That would be a nice touch. Maybe we can find you some sparklers to wave around."

I tried to think of some smart-alecky reply to throw

back at him, but he was right. Spies should never attract attention—unless they're doing it on purpose to distract people from secret actions being done by other spies.

"What's going on?"

"We have a chance to take out RABID from the very top," he said. "If we act now, we can cut the head off the snake. That would be a major step toward destroying them."

He definitely had my attention. I'd love to see RABID wiped out. The name stood for Raise Anarchy by Inciting Disorder. They wanted to control people by making them unhappy with their leaders. They were responsible for plenty of the bad things that happened in the world. They would have done even more bad things if Mr. Murphy and I hadn't been around to stop some of their plans.

"But you said they're too spread out to get rid of." From what I knew, RABID worked in little groups all around the world. Mr. Murphy called the groups *cells*.

"We think we know how to locate the man at the very top of the organization. If we can capture Baron von Lyssa, the cells won't survive for long." Mr. Murphy pulled a folded sheet of paper from his pocket and handed it to me. "Ever heard of this?"

I opened it up and read the first three lines.

BRAINY BRAWNY
Enter a Team in the Ultimate
Athletic and Academic Competition!

Below the headline, there was a drawing of a kid with a big head and bulging muscles. He had a dumbbell in one hand and a book in the other. The flyer looked sort of familiar. "I saw this on the bulletin board last month," I said. It had quickly gotten covered by posters about the band concert, the bake sale, and all sorts of other stuff. "They put up an announcement every year. Nobody from our school ever enters."

I noticed Abigail was staring at the flyer. Then her gaze drifted toward the clouds, like she was thinking about something.

"That kid must have to buy his hats somewhere special," Mookie said. "What's that have to do with us, anyhow?"

"We think RABID looks for exceptional young people and convinces them to join the organization. Sometimes, they start working on their candidates when they're years away from becoming active."

"And kids who enter the contest are more likely to have the sorts of skills that RABID would find useful," Abigail said. "Especially the winners."

"I've been told you're quite smart," Mr. Murphy said. "Apparently, that's the case. I assume you know what I'm going to ask next."

"Ooohhh! Let me guess!" Mookie raised his hand, like we were in class, waved it wildly, and then shouted out, "You want us to parachute out of a jet and attack the bad guys. Right?" He clenched his fists above his

MOORESVILLE PUBLIC LIBRARY
2215 WEST HARRISON STREET
MOORESVILLE, INDIANA 46158

shoulders, the way people do when they're hanging under a parachute. Then he tugged down with his left fist and skittered in that direction.

Mr. Murphy made a face like he'd just tried to swallow a large slice of moldy onion. "Well, lad, I wouldn't mind dropping you out of a jet, preferably over an empty stretch of ocean, but that's not exactly the current plan. Though I'll keep it in mind for later, should an opportunity arise."

"No jet?" Mookie asked.

"No jet," Mr. Murphy said.

"He wants us to form a team, enter the competition, and do well enough that we're approached by RABID," Abigail said. "That's why he's talking to all three of us. Each Brainy Brawny team has three people on it."

"That was my next guess," Mookie said. "But I didn't want to show off too much. Nobody likes a smarty-pants. Or a smarty-skirt."

"Correct again." Mr. Murphy nodded at Abigail, who happened to be wearing a skirt today.

"Okay, so you want us to enter the contest," I said. "I guess we have a chance to do well. But why didn't you just send a message to me like you usually do?"

"There wasn't time. We figured out RABID's connection with Brainy Brawny late this morning, right before the sign-up deadline. All three of you need to fill out an entry form immediately." He handed each of us a sheet of paper and a pen. "Fill these out, and I'll mail them right away. But before you do, I need to make sure all of you understand what you're getting into."

"A jet?" Mookie asked.

I had a good idea I knew what Mr. Murphy meant. "We'll be meeting with a very dangerous person. At some point, we might be on our own, out of touch with BUM. If we mess up, there won't be anyone to come to our rescue."

"Exactly," Mr. Murphy said. "Wherever you go to meet him, you'll be scanned for electronic devices, so we can't use any sort of tracker or beacon. You'll be isolated. They'll take steps to make sure you aren't being followed. We'll have no way to communicate. If they suspect you, bad things could happen. There are definite dangers. The choice is yours."

"I'm in," Abigail said.

"Me, too," Mookie said. "Can I keep the pen?"

"Looks like we have a competition to win." I checked out the entry form. "Our parents don't have to sign anything?"

"Not for the local competition at your school," Mr. Murphy said. "You'll need permission for the regional competitions, but I'm sure that won't be a problem."

I filled out the form and handed it back to Mr. Murphy.

He put the sheets in an envelope. "You're doing a good thing—all three of you. I'll be in touch very soon." He nodded at us, then walked off.

"I guess we'd better start practicing," Mookie said. "Do you think there'll be lots of math?"

"You can't practice for this," Abigail said. "We could be asked to do anything."

"I can practice spying." Mookie squatted, squinted, and looked around from side to side. "I know we'll be doing that."

"Good grief!" Abigail backed away from Mookie and fanned the air in front of her nose. "Don't squat around people. It puts too much pressure on your overloaded intestines."

"Sorry." Mookie shrugged and stood up. "Oops. Sorry again. I guess getting up from a squat presses on stuff, too. But I can't help it if my intestines are overloaded. Mom made her cauliflower casserole last night. The recipe takes three whole cans of spray cheese. It's too good to resist."

Abigail backed farther away from him. "I wonder whether they'll ask about current events? I haven't read today's newspaper yet. Or any of this week's news magazines. I'd better get going."

"I thought you just told us we can't prepare for this," I said.

"We can't. But it doesn't hurt to brush up on a topic or two, just in case. I gotta go." She dashed several steps away, then stopped when the opening notes of the Jupiter Symphony played from her purse. That was her current favorite ringtone. I wouldn't have known the name if she hadn't told me. Last month, she'd used the nesting call of the speckled grackle.

She pulled her phone from her purse, spoke for a moment, then ran back to me.

"Nathan!" she said. "There's amazing news!"

2

Making a Pig of Myself

What?" **I had** no clue who could be calling Abigail with important news.

"Let me guess," Mookie said. "Mr. Murphy called because he changed his mind about the jet." He held his arms out like wings and ran in swooping circles around us, making jet engine whooshes. Then he shouted, "Uh-oh! Eject! Eject! Mayday!" He leaped in the air and did the parachute thing again.

"That was Dr. Cushing," Abigail said. "She told me she finally solved the last problem with the bone machine."

"For real?" That was amazingly good news. I'd been

waiting forever for her to fix the machine. My bones are weak, because I'm dead. Dr. Cushing, who works for BUM, built a machine that could strengthen my bones. It worked fine when she tested it on my hand. But when she'd boosted the power so it could do my whole body, the first version had some bad, and messy, side effects.

After blowing up the test subject, Dr. Cushing, who's pretty brilliant herself, joined forces with Abigail, who's a science genius. They'd been trying all sorts of things to make the machine safe.

"For real," Abigail said. "We'd been exploring the whole resonance problem, and she thought up a different approach last week, involving harmonics. We used Fourier transformations to create sine waves—"

I held up my hand to stop her. I realized she was excited, but she might as well have been barking or meowing. The words didn't mean a thing. "It works?"

"Yup, it works," Abigail said. "Everything is all set. You should go there right now."

"Do you want to come?" I asked.

"They won't let me in," she said. "You know how strict they are about security. But we can wait for you down the street from the museum, like we used to do back when BUM first approached you."

"That would be great."

"I wish they'd let us inside," Mookie said. "I'll bet it's awesome."

"Yeah, too bad they won't," I said. It would be nice

having my friends there with me. But I could just see Mookie stumbling across the room at the wrong time, banging into the bone machine, and changing the way it worked so I ended up with a gigantic head like the kid on the Brainy Brawny flyer. Or maybe I'd end up with flexible bones and antlers. As if I didn't already have enough problems with my body. The one lucky thing about being half-dead was that nobody could tell it just by looking at me. At least, not yet.

Mookie and Abigail walked through town with me toward the Museum of Tile and Grout. The secret entrance to get from our town of East Craven to BUM headquarters was in the lobby of the museum. BUM had secret entrances all over the place.

"You're so lucky," Mookie said while we waited for a light to change.

"Are you kidding?"

"Nope. I'm totally serious. Most people are scared about all kinds of stuff. Look at Ferdinand. He's afraid of everything. Even I'm scared of some stuff, and I'm pretty brave most of the time. But you—you have nothing to worry about. Nothing bad can happen. If you cut off a hand, you can just glue it back on. If there's a poisonous gas leak, you won't even notice. You have no worries."

I looked across the street at a construction site. They were pouring concrete. I imagined what would happen if I fell into it when nobody was around to help me out.

A regular person would die. But not me. I didn't need to breathe. So I'd be stuck there, sealed in, trapped forever, with nothing for company except my thoughts and memories. Mookie was wrong. It's not that I had no worries. I had different worries. And lots of them.

"Am I right?" Mookie asked.

I couldn't tell him what had just gone through my mind. It would only add to his own list of nightmares. "Yeah. You're right. In some ways, I guess I'm pretty lucky."

"Speaking of that, good luck," Abigail said.

I realized we'd reached the museum.

"Break a leg," Mookie said.

"I already did that. It wasn't fun."

Abigail's phone beeped. I hoped there wasn't a problem. "It's a text," she said. "But not from Dr. Cushing. I don't recognize the number."

I looked at the display.

HUNTING CUR

MOREL EATER

"This makes no sense," Abigail said. "A cur is a dog, and a morel is a mushroom. Who cares if a hunting dog eats mushrooms? It must be a wrong number, or some kind of glitch. Never mind. You'd better get going." She shoved the phone back in her purse.

"Yeah. Here I go." I went inside and took the

elevator—which was really more like a rocket car—to BUM headquarters.

Mr. Murphy was waiting for me on the other side. "Well, it looks like you're no longer going to be able to claim the title of the world's most breakable spy."

"Yeah," I said. "I guess you'll have to find other reasons to make fun of me."

"That shouldn't prove very challenging. You're an endless source of inspiration. Come on, let's go stiffen your spine."

I followed Mr. Murphy to Dr. Cushing's lab. "Nathan," she said when I walked in, "I'm so happy we got the machine working."

There was a large vat of milk on the floor, beneath the latest version of the bone machine. I tried to figure out how the machine was different from before, but I really had no idea what I was looking at. It was just a bunch of wires, metal parts, glass tubes, switches, and dials.

I pointed at the vat. "Do I get in now?"

"Not yet. I wanted you to see the final test for yourself, first," Dr. Cushing said. "It's all set to go."

"Thanks. It'll be nice to know for sure that it works, before you try it on me," I said. "I remember the first time you fired this thing up."

"I think we all do. I still have nightmares where pig pieces rain from the sky." She shuddered. "But this will prove to you that everything is safe."

I watched as she flipped a switch on the side of the machine and turned a dial all the way to the right. Last time, the milk started bubbling like it was simmering on a stovetop. Then, the pig exploded. It wasn't a live pig, but it was still a juicy one. It was a good thing nothing can make me feel sick to my stomach, because that shower of pork parts would definitely have made me throw up for a solid week or two.

This time, the milk didn't even ripple as it filled with tiny bubbles. Better yet, the pig didn't blow up. The three of us—me, Dr. Cushing, and Mr. Murphy—stared at the perfectly calm surface of the milk as the liquid turned clear.

"All the calcium is getting absorbed by the bones," Dr. Cushing said. "Give me a hand, please, Peter."

"It works," I said as she and Mr. Murphy lifted the pig out of the vat. "This is great."

"And it's safe," she said. "Abigail and I went over the calculations a dozen times, just to make sure we didn't miss anything. But I'm not going to trust the calculations by themselves, even though the pig appears to be fine. I need an hour to run some tests on our subject, to make sure everything is okay. And I'll have to refill the vat."

Finally, I'd get my bones strengthened. That was great. I was tired of my fingers snapping off like over-baked pretzel rods. A brittle spy isn't anywhere near as useful as a sturdy spy.

Dr. Cushing started examining the pig. "I don't want to take any chances. I'll run a full set of tests."

"No point waiting here," Mr. Murphy said. "Come on, lad—let's find something more interesting to do for the next hour."

3

Odds and Ends

I followed Mr. Murphy out of the lab. "Hey, once my bones are strong, maybe someone here can teach me karate." I threw a punch at an imaginary enemy. "Every spy should know self-defense."

He laughed. He did that a lot. "I think I can find better ways for you to spend your training time. There are plenty of thugs and musclemen available. We need stealth and guile. You're a lurker, not a fighter."

"But why can't I be both? It would be so cool." I chopped at the air.

"Well, we certainly built this entire organization so you could have *cool* experiences," Mr. Murphy said. "After we teach you karate and how to drive a race car, would you like us to send you to the moon?"

I finished off my imaginary enemy with a kick. "Only if you promise I can strap you to the outside of the rocket."

Mr. Murphy laughed even louder. "It appears you don't have any need of karate. You already know how to defend yourself."

Instead of going to his office, we went to the room with the large video screen. Mr. Murphy pointed to the couch. "I want you to understand everything about this mission."

"No secrets?" I asked. Mr. Murphy didn't like to tell anyone anything unless they absolutely needed to know it.

"I never said that. There will always be secrets. But I want you to have enough background information so you'll do the right things when you're approached."

Before he could say anything more, a small intercom on the desk beeped.

"Go ahead," Mr. Murphy said.

"We need high-speed transport for three agents from Ulner Airfield," the voice said.

"Got it." Mr. Murphy turned toward me. "This will just take a moment." He went to a table by the wall, flipped open a laptop, and pulled up a website. He typed some stuff, then closed the laptop. "Okay, get comfortable. We have a lot to cover."

I plopped down on the couch while he picked up the remote and hit some buttons.

The screen divided into squares, like a checkerboard. "These are the RABID operatives we've identified, thanks to the work you've done." Faces popped into all the squares.

"That many?" I asked.

"It might seem like a lot, but we've uncovered only a small portion of them. There are far more still out there. But this isn't about numbers. It's about patterns." He pushed another button. "For example, let's divide them by age."

As I watched, the faces moved to different spots on the screen. I could see that the youngest ones were on the left and the oldest were on the right. "It looks pretty even," I said.

"Definitely. Age tells us nothing. Let's look at where they were born." He pushed a button. There was another shift. "Education." Another shift. "Voting record." He went through a dozen different categories.

"Nothing seems to mean anything special," I said.

"Correct." Mr. Murphy lowered the remote. "Because this is the wrong way to analyze the information. I could spend years trying to think up the right connection and never come close. Let's reverse the approach, and have the computer search for common links that occur at unusual levels."

I wasn't totally sure what that meant, but I figured Mr. Murphy would explain it.

The faces faded away, along with the squares. Words and numbers flashed across the screen. Each one flickered on just long enough for me to read it. I noticed words like COLLEGE, AUTOMOBILE, and SIBLINGS. Then one set of words flashed on and stayed there: BRAINY BRAWNY.

More words and some numbers showed up under that line:

Participation in BRAINY BRAWNY competition

7 of the 64

Portion of group: 10.9%

Probability: .005%

I stared at Mr. Murphy. "It was just seven of them. Why's that a big deal?"

"Seven out of sixty-four. As you see, that's more than one out of every ten. How many people that you know have competed in Brainy Brawny?" he asked.

"None, until now."

He nodded. "If you grabbed a thousand people at random, how many do you think would have ever been in Brainy Brawny?"

"I don't know. A couple?"

"Right. A couple. At most. Think about it. Finding seven in a group of sixty-four would be like finding out that over one hundred of those thousand had been in it."

I wasn't as good with numbers as Abigail, but I started to see what he meant. It's hard to imagine even one or two people out of any random group of a thousand might have entered Brainy Brawny. But seven of the sixty-four RABID agents that BUM uncovered had been in it. That was a lot. And that was just from the agents we knew about. "So that's the pattern," I said. "That's how you know RABID gets people from Brainy Brawny."

"Exactly." Mr. Murphy hit another button. "Then we worked from the other direction. We analyzed every person who'd ever participated in Brainy Brawny, and graphed that against any sort of criminal involvement later in life. We figured some of RABID's operatives would have been caught doing something bad, even if they weren't linked with RABID at the time they were arrested. They do some pretty evil things."

I looked at the graph. "Wow. I can see why you want me to enter Brainy Brawny."

"And to get recruited by Baron von Lyssa."

"What's he look like?" I asked.

"We don't know. Not yet. Right now, all we know is his name. But we'll know much more about him as soon as your Brainy Brawny performance draws him to you. And you'll have helped deal a crippling blow to RABID. As I said, without him, they'll be like a snake without a head. They might writhe and wriggle for a while, but eventually they'll die. And that, lad, is enough, all by itself, to make everything we've done to get to this point worthwhile."

"Can't you just grab him when he comes to watch the contest?"

"That would certainly make things easier," Mr. Murphy said. "But Baron von Lyssa would never go to the competition. He'll just wait until the results are made public. He probably won't even approach you, himself, for the first contact. The man takes no risks. But he also doesn't let anyone else do the recruiting. You can be sure, once a meeting is arranged, that he'll be there. And so will we."

A moment later, Dr. Cushing called us back to the lab. When we got there, she handed me a bathing suit. "No point getting your clothes wet."

"Thanks." I went to a bathroom down the hall and changed. On the way back to the lab, I kept thinking about the messy moment when the first pig had exploded. I could understand why Dr. Cushing still had nightmares. But I trusted her. And I really trusted Abigail. She'd never put me in danger.

"It might tingle a little," Dr. Cushing said as I stepped into the vat of milk.

"If it makes my bones stronger, I don't care if it burns." I leaned back in the vat and let my body sink below the surface. I heard a click as Dr. Cushing threw a switch. Then I heard a hum. My whole body started to tingle. I'm glad she'd warned me about that. My fingers grew warm—just like when Dr. Cushing had run the machine on my hand. So did my toes. The tingle spread to my arms and legs, and then to my whole body. I liked it.

The milk around me filled with tiny bubbles. If I'd been able to feel them, I'm sure the bubbles would have tickled. The milk grew clearer. Finally, after a couple of minutes, the milk was as clear as water. The tingles faded. The hum of the machine grew fainter, then died completely.

I looked over at Dr. Cushing. She nodded and waved a hand to let me know it was okay to get out.

I sat up and clenched my fist. It was hard to tell if there was any difference in my bones. I grabbed my little finger and bent it. It didn't break. I pulled at my wrist. My arm felt strong. "I think it worked."

"So do I." Dr. Cushing handed me a towel. "There's a shower room down the hall to the left, just around the corner."

"Thanks." I toweled myself off enough to stop the dripping, then grabbed my clothes and headed for the shower.

Strong bones.

That was great. Of course, I was still dead, and slowly rotting. I stared at my fingers. They were pale and flaky. I'd seen healthier flesh spread out on the crushed ice in the fish market. I checked my face in the mirror. It was pretty pale, too. But this was the first time since I'd been splashed with Hurt-Be-Gone that any part of my half-dead condition had improved. One problem at a time, I guess.

When I got back to the lab, Dr. Cushing tapped my nose with her forefinger, and then my ear. "Remember, some parts of you aren't bone. So don't go trying to be Superman."

"I'll remember."

Mr. Murphy held up a padded box with a small dial in the upper corner. "Punch this," he said. "It will measure how strong your bones are."

"Will it explode?" I asked. A lot of BUM's devices seemed to blow up when they weren't supposed to.

"Stop being so tedious. It's not even electronic."

I hauled off and socked it. The box shattered. Mr. Murphy looked down at the broken pieces on the floor. "It seems your bones are even stronger than we'd expected."

"That was the one possible side effect Abigail and I discussed," Dr. Cushing said. "Though it's obviously not a harmful one."

"Not harmful to *me*." I flexed my fingers and stared at my fist. The skin over my knuckles looked a little flattened. I squeezed it back into shape. It felt sort of squishy, like grapes that had fallen into the bottom of the fridge and stayed there for a month or two. Even so, this was definitely an interesting development. Who'd have guessed a dead kid could end up with a powerful punch. "This is pretty lucky timing. Strong bones could come in handy during the tournament," I said.

Something flickered across Mr. Murphy's face. But then he smiled and said, "I suspect it might."

With Mr. Murphy, I always assumed he had secrets. I wondered what he wasn't telling me.

Enter the Bully

Abigail and Mookie met me as soon as I left the museum.

"Well?" she asked.

"How'd it go?" Mookie asked.

"Not good." I limped a couple of steps, then screamed in pain and dropped to my knees. I wrapped my arms around my chest and shuddered like I was in danger of falling apart. Mookie's eyes got wide, but Abigail didn't fall for it.

"Nice try," she said. "I guess it's safe to assume the machine worked."

"Yeah. It worked perfectly. Better than perfectly." I

got back up. "My bones are stronger than ever. Watch this."

I walked over to a parking meter and punched it. The meter vibrated on its pole like it had been whacked with a baseball bat.

"Cool!" Mookie said.

"Careful," Abigail said. "Your bones are stronger, but your skin still can't heal."

"Good point." I realized I couldn't go around hitting things all the time. I didn't want my bones popping through my skin.

"Even so, I'm happy for you," Abigail said.

"And we don't have to worry about you snapping in half anymore," Mookie said. "You can stop carrying your glue around."

"No way." I patted my pocket. I never left the house without a bottle of the glue. "My bones are stronger, but they could still break. Right?"

"Right," Abigail said. "It would just take a lot of force. I think it would be smart to keep carrying the glue."

We headed down the street. "You sure you're okay with the idea of entering this contest?" I asked Abigail. "People will find out you're smart." She'd kept her intelligence a secret ever since she'd been badly kidded about it when she was little. Even our friends at our lunch table had no idea Abigail was beyond brilliant.

"It'll be fine," Abigail said. "We won't be competing

at Belgosi. Nobody at school will ever find out about me."

Abigail might be really smart, but as we all found out the next day, she definitely couldn't see into the future.

We were sitting in science class when the loudspeaker crackled. "The following students please report to the office: Nathan Abercrombie, Hutner Vetch, Abigail Goldberg, Rodney Mullasco, Eddy Mason, and Mort Platner."

Mookie thumped his desk. "I hate when they call me that." His mom and dad had planned to call him Hunter, but they'd messed up the name at the hospital and never bothered to fix it.

"I wonder what this is about?" I said as we got up from our seats. I knew I wasn't in trouble. And I definitely wasn't part of anything that involved Rodney. He was a bully. Eddy was pretty mean, too. He also thought he was the smartest kid in the school. I loved knowing how totally wrong he was about that. Mort was nice enough. He was a great athlete.

"Wait a minute . . . ," I said as we walked down the hall. *Smart kid . . . athletic kid . . . strong kid . . .*

Click—click—click. The pieces fell together before we reached the office. I looked over at Abigail. She nodded. I could tell she was thinking the same thing. She'd probably figured it out way before I did.

When we went up to the counter in the main office,

the secretary pointed to the conference room. I took a seat at the large rectangular table. We were the first ones there. Mookie and Abigail sat on either side of me.

I noticed dark crumbs scattered in front of us. Mookie pressed his index finger into some of them, sniffed it, then said, "Brownies. Yum."

I grabbed his wrist before he could lick his finger. "You don't know how old they are."

"Hey, stale brownies are awesome." Mookie looked around. "I wonder if there's any ice cream. Sometimes they have a little refrigerator in these rooms."

Speaking of crumbs, that's when Rodney, Mort, and Eddy showed up. They sat on the other side of the table. That was good. I liked staying as far from Rodney as possible.

"If you told on me, I'll hurt you," Rodney said to us.

"Told about what?" I asked.

He just glared. I stared back. That was easy. I don't need to blink. Rodney blinked once or twice, but he didn't look away. I guess he was too stupid to realize he'd been outstared. Finally, he said, "There's something creepy about you."

Just then, Principal Ambrose walked in, carrying some sheets of paper in one hand and a thick booklet in the other. He looked tired. But he always looked that way. He was retiring at the end of the school year. I wondered whether *tired* and *retired* had anything to do with each other. Either way, he was ready to go. I'd heard he had a big calendar in his office, where he crossed off each day as soon as the last bell rang.

He raised one hand and waved the sheets of paper at us as he walked to the head of the table. "It seems we have two teams entering the Brainy Brawny competition this year."

The six of us exchanged a variety of glances. Rodney smirked. Eddy laughed. Mort shrugged. None of us spoke in words, but we still seemed to be having a conversation.

Of course, when it came to conversations, Rodney's favorite topic was always something along the lines of, *You're dead,* or *I'm going to win.* And everything Eddy said pretty much really just meant, *I'm smarter than you are,* or *You're stupid.*

"Nobody from this school has ever entered before," Principal Ambrose said. "Not one single team, in all the years I've been here."

"Cool," Mookie said. "We're the first. You must be proud of us. I've always been sort of adventurous." He grinned at the principal. "We should celebrate. Got any ice cream?"

Principal Ambrose glared at him with enough force that Mookie—who was usually glare proof—wriggled in his seat.

"The first round is run by the school." Principal Ambrose paused, as if waiting for his words to sink in. Then he lifted up his other hand and showed us the booklet. "Someone here has to be in charge of this thing. There are a lot of rules and guidelines. Far too many rules." He opened his hand and let the booklet drop. It smacked against the table like a five-pound bag of flour.

Okay. Now I got it. He didn't want the extra work. He might be here until June, but I think he'd already stopped caring about the job.

"Of course, if one team drops out, there's no need for the school to run anything." He stared directly at me, Mookie, and Abigail. "Since this is a contest for the smartest, strongest, and fittest, I think the choice is obvious. Three of you can save yourselves from an embarrassing defeat by dropping out now."

I heard Rodney snicker. But I didn't take my eyes off Principal Ambrose. I could outstare anyone, not just bullies like Rodney.

After a moment, the principal glanced back down at the rules. "I don't think the other teachers who'll have to get involved will be all that happy about spending hours creating a contest for just two teams. Especially when one team doesn't have a chance. No chance at all."

Another stare.

Another snicker.

"I'm sure Mr. Lomux will be especially unhappy." Principal Ambrose flipped open the rule manual. "Each contest needs a physical education specialist, as well as a science teacher and a language arts teacher. No, I fear Mr. Lomux will not appreciate this at all."

Mr. Lomux? Oh, boy. That was going to make things more complicated. He was so mean, he was almost like an adult version of Rodney. He would have been even more dangerous if he wasn't stuck with a brain about as powerful as the sort you'd find in the average earthworm.

"That's bad," Mookie whispered. "Remember what he did to us with the socks?"

"Yeah," I whispered back. "That was pretty brutal." After we'd annoyed him by not acting like "real men," he'd made the whole gym class put our dirty socks over our noses and breathe through them.

"So," Principal Ambrose said, "there's absolutely no disgrace in deciding to withdraw from the competition."

"No thanks," I said. "We're in it to win."

Rodney and Eddy both started laughing. Mort didn't laugh, but I could see from his smile that he thought his team would have a very easy time beating us. And they would—if we were actually who they thought we were. But everything they thought was wrong.

They thought Abigail was just some spooky kid who didn't talk much in class. They thought I was a decent athlete, but not as good as they were. Sure, I'd won a field day event last fall, but that memory had faded. Or maybe they didn't think chin-ups meant all that much. I guess, in a way, I really couldn't argue with them. It was hard for me to think of myself as a good athlete, when I knew I was dead. But my muscles never got tired, and I never ran out of breath. I guess that gave me a big advantage in anything that needed endurance.

Either way, they didn't really have a clue what Abigail and I could do. As for Mookie, they had no idea how tough he could be. He might act like a total goofball, but if I asked him to hang from a rope by his teeth, he'd find a way to do it, and he'd hang on as long as he had to. Unless, of course, he opened his mouth to shout something like, "Don't worry! I'll never open my mouth."

"Last chance . . . ," Principal Ambrose said. "I'll see that you still get nice certificates for second place. And you won't have to add to your teachers' workloads or go through the humiliation of losing."

I didn't even bother answering.

"All right. Have it your way," he said. "Go back to your classes."

Rodney bumped me on the way out. I thought about slugging him with my extra-hard fist. But I didn't want to get in trouble. More important than that, I didn't want him to suspect there was anything unusual about me. I probably shouldn't have stared at him for so long without blinking. Luckily, his brain power, and his memory, were pretty much like Mr. Lomux's.

"Well, that was a waste of everyone's time," Abigail said.

"No way. Look what I got." Mookie held up a small

brown lump. "I made a whole piece of brownie from the crumbs. Anyone want a bite?"

"Anyone want bacteria?" Abigail said.

"It's all yours," I said.

As we walked back to our classroom, I noticed that Rodney was heading toward the gym. "Great," I said. "He's going to let Mr. Lomux know what's happening."

"They're probably going to plan some way to make us lose," Abigail said.

"Or hurt us," I said. Not that I could feel pain. But stronger bones or not, I could still get damaged.

Then I realized there was an even bigger problem. "Oh, no!" I spun toward Abigail. "You know what this means?"

"I'm way ahead of you," she said.

"I'm not," Mookie said. "I'm never ahead of you. I have no idea what you two are talking about. What's going on?"

5

So Much for Secrets

If we have our first round of the Brainy Brawny competition here at Belgosi, kids will find out how smart Abigail is," I said.

"Hey, that shouldn't be a problem. We know how smart she is, and we like her," Mookie said. "Even if she's smarter than anyone really needs to be."

"It's not the same. We've been through all sorts of stuff together. We know her better than anyone." I looked over at Abigail. If she'd been some stranger who raised her hand all the time and knew all the answers, I might feel differently about her. But together, we'd faced life, death, and a very messy flock of seagulls. We'd even tackled an eighth-grade bully—and lived to laugh about it.

"It's up to you, Abigail. Mr. Murphy can't force you to do this. And you've worked really hard to keep your secret all these years. Things can stay the way they are, if that's what you want."

"I want to do this," Abigail said. "It's important to help BUM. And you know what—I'm tired of hiding the truth. Deception has become too large a part of my life."

"I sure know what you mean. It's hard when your whole life is wrapped up in hiding stuff." I spent a ton of energy keeping the truth from everyone. I pretended to eat, so my parents wouldn't worry. I even pretended to go to the bathroom, because my mom paid far too much attention to stuff like that. Half my life was a lie, and the other half was spent spying.

Sometimes, late at night, when I had too much free time to fill and couldn't help thinking about stuff, I wasn't even sure who I really was anymore. But unlike Abigail, I didn't think I could deal with having everyone know my secret. People would run away from me if they knew I was a zombie.

"Hey," Mookie said. "What's my secret? You and Abigail have secrets. I gotta have something. I'm good at bowling, but that isn't a secret." He took a couple steps and threw an imaginary ball.

"Well, you have the power to turn just about anything from a solid into a gas, merely by swallowing it," I said.

"That's no secret," Abigail said. "That's general knowledge, with frequent reminders. Sometimes I'm amazed that you don't float."

"Maybe your secret is so secret, even you don't know it," I said.

"Yeah," Mookie said. "I'll bet you're right."

"Speaking of secrets," Abigail said, "I think you might be able to back me up for the academic part of Brainy Brawny."

"Me? I'm not all that great when it comes to knowing stuff."

"Maybe not when you were alive. But I have a theory. Here—this will just take a moment." Abigail reached into her purse and pulled out a deck of cards.

"You just happened to have those with you?" I asked.

"No. I brought them specifically for this. Watch closely." She held the deck up, with the cards facing me, then put her thumb on top and riffled through the deck so each card flashed past."

"Are you doing some kind of magic trick?" Mookie asked.

"Nope," she said, turning the back of the deck toward me. "Nathan is."

"What are you talking about?" I knew only one card trick, and I could never do it right.

"Tell me the first card you saw," she said.

"Ten of hearts." That was easy. It was the front card.

"Right." Abigail pulled the ten from the deck and showed it to me, then dropped it into her purse. "Next card?"

"Not a clue."

"Just take a guess."

"King of clubs?"

"Right." She turned the whole deck toward me to show the king, then turned it away and pulled the king off. "Keep going."

"Six of spades?"

"Right."

"Nine of hearts?"

"Yup."

I got the whole deck without a single mistake. "How'd I do that?" I asked when she showed me the last card.

"I'm not positive, but I have a theory," she said.

"That makes one of us. I don't have a clue."

"Our brains have short-term and long-term memories. Stuff we don't need gets tossed out. At least, that's what most scientists believe. But your brain is dead. I had a suspicion it would keep everything. What did I have for lunch yesterday?"

"Chicken sandwich, fruit cup, and seven chocolate Kisses." I couldn't believe I knew that.

"What did I have?" Mookie asked.

"That's too easy. You had one of everything," I said.

"But how does this help with Brainy Brawny? They aren't going to be asking what we had for lunch."

"That's true. But they might ask stuff in an area where I'm not strong. I know—I'll make you a reading list."

"Sure. It's not like I have a ton of stuff to do at night."

We went back into science class and took our seats. As I listened to the lesson, I imagined what it would be like if Abigail didn't have to hide her brains. She was so smart, and so excited about knowledge, she really wanted to share everything. Maybe this would be good for her.

AS we were leaving school, Abigail's phone beeped. "Not again. I keep getting these weird texts." She held up the phone.

RARF LOWER

"That's not how you spell *barf*," Mookie said.

"That's not how you spell anything meaningful." Abigail turned off her phone and dropped it into her purse. "I'll see you guys later. I have to go do something with my mom."

Mookie was free, so he walked home with me. "I got it!" he said right before we reached my house.

"I hope it's not catching," I said.

"No, seriously—I just figured out how to bring you back to life. Remember Frankenstein?"

"Sure." I'd watched that movie once. It was really old, but it was sort of cool.

"The monster was all dead, right? He was just a bunch of stitched-together dead parts, until he got zapped with electricity. That brought him to life."

"We already tried electricity. Remember? You zapped me with that defibrillator when we figured out my heart wasn't beating." That seemed like so long ago. I could still remember lying down in Mr. Lomux's office while Mookie zapped me with a zillion volts.

"But that was just a little jolt," he said. "The monster needed lightning. We have to figure out how to get you hit by a big bolt of lightning. Hey, I've got a kite. Isn't that what Ben Franklin used?"

"Are you trying to get me killed?" As the last word left my mouth, I realized it didn't make sense. But there had to be a word for it.

I guess Mookie had the same thought. "You mean killdered?" he said. "Wait—killderd. No, that doesn't sound right. Deader. That's it." He grinned. "Nope. I'm not trying to make you deader. I'm trying to unkill you."

"Either way, it won't work," I said. "I got zapped by an electric fence, too, and that didn't bring me back to life. Electricity isn't the answer."

When we reached my porch, Mookie stopped, wrinkled his nose, and looked around. "Speaking of electricity, I think a squirrel just got zapped by a power line."

"Oh, no." I guess Mom had come home early and decided to cook. She does that once in a while. I went inside and headed for the kitchen to see how bad it was.

There were pots everywhere. I sniffed. The house smelled like the bottom of the charcoal grill after it's been sitting around outside all winter.

"You're just in time. I made chili. It came out great." Mom dipped a tablespoon in the pot, then thrust the spoon at my face. "Here, taste."

I was going to say I was full. But Mom looked so proud, I couldn't let her down. I opened my mouth and leaned forward.

"Chili!" Mookie pushed me aside and clamped his mouth onto the spoon. "Mmmmmmm," he said with his lips still around the spoon. He stepped back, chewed, swallowed, then said, "Delicious. This is the best chili I've had all day."

"I'm so glad you like it." Mom opened the cabinet door above the sink. "I'll get you boys a bowl."

"Not now," I said. "I'm still pretty full from lunch." I edged my way toward the hall. "But it smells great. Really great."

"I'll have some," Mookie said. "Better give me a bowl for Nathan. He could get hungry later." He got two bowls of chili from Mom and took them up to my room. "It definitely tastes better than it smells."

"Thanks for saving me," I said.

"No problem. Maybe I get a little gas once in a while, but the stuff you cook up in your gut can kill people. The chicken wings were bad enough. I'd hate to think what would happen with chili."

"Me, too. But I can't keep this up forever," I said. "Sooner or later, they're going to figure out something is wrong with me."

"I don't know," Mookie said. "Parents don't pay that much attention to kids. I got stuck at the top of that tree in my backyard last year, and my parents didn't even notice until the next morning. They were having some sort of ceramic-angels shopping marathon on TV, so Mom was pretty wrapped up. Dad never notices anything."

"Yeah, my dad's like that, too." I felt my cheek. When anyone drew zombies in comic books or in movie ads, it was always the cheekbones that stuck out first. "But what happens when pieces of me start to fall off?"

"I guess they might notice that. But you're not falling apart yet, are you?"

"Nope." I pushed my finger against my arm. The skin felt soft.

"So stop worrying. Things will work out." Mookie finished his bowl of chili and started working on mine. "Can I stay for dinner?"

"Sure."

"It will be chili, right?"

"I'm afraid so."

Mookie had three more bowls that evening before he headed home. After dinner, I decided to test my memory. I grabbed the first volume of the encyclopedia from the bookcase in the living room and opened it at random. I read an article about a plant I'd never heard of, called *agony vera*. It had sharp needles that caused extreme itching.

I closed the book and tried to see what I could remember. It was all there, like I was still looking at the page. Every fact about the plant was right in front of me. This was sort of cool. But it was also scary. Everyone I knew was always running out of storage space in their game systems. Would my brain run out of memory if I filled it? Was there some way I could delete the extra stuff? I didn't want to think too hard about that right now.

The next morning, I asked Abigail, "Do you have that reading list?"

She gave me a funny smile.

"What's wrong?"

"I tried to think of an area where you could back me up, and there's really nothing. I'm not good at sports trivia, but they won't ask that in an academic competition. I think I've got everything covered. I'm sorry."

"Don't forget me," Mookie said. "I know lots of stuff,

too. I can back up Abigail. You can just concentrate on the dead-kid stuff."

That was fine with me. It was fun knowing I had this special memory, but it was nice to know I didn't have to worry about that part of the competition.

It looked like there was something else I wouldn't have to worry about. During morning announcements, the secretary said, "Be sure to come to the gym on Saturday morning for the first-ever Brainy Brawny showdown at Belgosi. Come root for your favorite team."

"Saturday morning," I said to Abigail. "That's perfect. Nobody will show up."

"I agree," she said. "I was afraid they'd hold the competition after school, when there were still kids hanging around. Or, worse, during school. If they'd had an assembly, we'd have the whole school staring at us. This is better. We're going to be fine."

"Definitely." I couldn't imagine any kids would bother to come to school on a weekend morning to watch some competition most of them had never heard of or cared about. "There's no reason anyone would show up. We'll be fine."

I hadn't counted on Rodney's need to have a large audience watch him crush his victims. The next day, there were posters taped up all over the hallways in school. Most of them had stuff like:

COME ROOT FOR RODNEY, EDDY, AND MORT

For some reason, there was a picture of the Roman Colosseum on most of them. That's the place where gladiators slaughtered each other. A couple of posters had extra stuff like, WATCH US DESTROY THE COMPETITION or SEE THE WEAKER TEAM GET STOMPED.

Since *competition* wasn't misspelled, I had a feeling Eddy had helped make the posters.

"It still won't make a difference," Abigail said as we stood in the hall near our home base, staring at a poster that promised, THERE WILL BE BLOOD! That one got taken down by a teacher before the end of the day.

"I hope you're right," I said.

She was wrong.

6

Team Spirit

Saturday morning, Mookie showed up at my house an hour before the competition. "I made us team uniforms." He held up a T-shirt. It was bright yellow, with black handwritten letters that read, *Team Mookie*.

"Team Mookie?" I asked.

"Well, it's good to use a name. And you have to admit, Team Nathan doesn't sound all that cool, and Team Abigail sounds like it has something to do with knitting." He handed me the shirt. "Put it on. Then we can go give Abigail hers."

"It's extra large," I said.

"They come in three-packs. I had to settle for one size. Small and medium don't work for me. Neither does large. I figured you and Abigail wouldn't mind a bit of extra room."

"She's never going to wear one," I said.

"Sure she will," Mookie said. "She's got team spirit. Put your shirt on, and we'll go over there."

I switched shirts. It was easier than arguing. The Team Mookie one hung on me like a small tent.

We headed over to Abigail's house.

She stared at us when Mookie held up the shirt. "No way."

"But we're a team," Mookie said. "Nathan's wearing his."

Abigail glared at me. Then she grabbed the shirt out of Mookie's hands. "I'm wearing a sweater over it." She ran off to change. When she came back, I could just see a little bit of the collar of a yellow T-shirt under her sweater. But it wasn't the same shade of yellow. I couldn't blame her.

"Do you feel ready for this?" she asked as we walked toward the school.

"I hope so. We have to win. It's not just about the contest. I don't care about that. It's about bringing down RABID."

"And Rodney," Mookie said. "I love seeing him lose."

"That's what I'm worried about," I said. "No matter

how bad he might be at figuring stuff out, he has to have noticed that I'm right there every time he has a disaster in his life. I've been around for Mr. Lomux's disasters, too."

Mookie laughed. "That was so awesome when Mr. Lomux and the middle school gym teacher got sick all over each other."

"I'd bet they don't feel that way," I said.

"Almost as cool as when you spewed a stomachful of rotting food all over Rodney," Mookie said.

"Almost." I guess nothing would top that for amazing moments. But I was afraid Rodney and Mr. Lomux had figured out I was bad luck for them, and had cooked up some sort of plan to get even. For people like them, getting even meant getting violent. I guessed I'd find out soon enough.

Right after we left Abigail's house, her phone beeped. She sighed, pulled it out, and checked the message.

"Oh, yuck!" she said. "That's just disgusting."

"Let me see." Mookie snatched the phone from her.

I looked over his shoulder at the message.

ENIMA FLOW!!!

"Definitely gross," I said.

"In a cool sort of way," Mookie said.

"That does it. I'm getting a new phone." Abigail grabbed the phone back from Mookie, turned it off, and shoved it in her purse.

When we reached the gym, I stopped by the doorway and stared at the bleachers. "This can't be the right place. Maybe there's supposed to be a basketball game or something." I looked at the scoreboard, but it was dark.

The gym was mobbed. There were tons of kids in the bleachers. Lots of parents, too. Including my own.

What are they doing here?

Dad waved at me. Mom held up a sign with my name on it.

"How'd they know about this?" I asked Abigail.

"No idea," she said.

"They probably saw it in the paper this morning," Mookie said.

"It was in the paper?"

"Sure," Mookie said. "I called them up and told them about it. I've never had my name in the paper. This seemed like it would be my only chance."

Abigail spun toward him, opened her mouth, then shrugged, sighed, and closed it.

Mookie turned to the bleachers and shouted, "Team Mookie has arrived!"

Principal Ambrose was standing by a pair of folding tables that were set up near center court. Mr. Lomux, dressed in his usual sweat clothes, was next to him, along with Ms. Delambre and Ms. Otranto. Each table had three buzzers on it, all hooked together by wires. There was a microphone stand in front of the tables.

Rodney, Eddy, and Mort were already sitting at one

of the tables. They had a big posterboard sign in front of the table, with THE BELGOSI BASHERS on it.

"I forgot to make a sign," Mookie said.

"What a shame," Abigail said.

Mookie pointed to the bleachers. "We could borrow your mom's sign and add the rest of our names."

"That's okay," I said. "Everyone already knows who we are."

"Everyone . . ." Abigail turned away from the bleachers, but then looked over her shoulder. "That's a big crowd."

We sat down at the other table. "You can't hold back," I told her. "We need all the points we can get."

"I know. Don't worry—if I'm going to do it at all, I'm going to give it my best."

Principal Ambrose let out a sigh even bigger than Abigail's, then walked to the microphone. He held up a note card and started to read from it. "Welcome to the local-level Brainy Brawny competition, featuring two teams from Belgosi Upper Elementary."

Buzzzz!!!

The sound bounced off the walls. It was like a gigantic bee had invaded the gym.

"Cool!" Mookie lifted his finger from the buzzer. "It works."

"Are you finished?" Principal Ambrose asked.

"Yup," Mookie said.

"Good," Principal Ambrose said. "Now, let's—"

Buzzz!!!

The principal glared at Mookie, who'd reached out and pressed my buzzer.

"Oops. Sorry. Now I'm finished," Mookie said. "I just wanted to make sure it worked every time. Wait—hang on." He leaned over farther and pressed Abigail's buzzer. "Okay—we're good. Go ahead."

Principal Ambrose read out our names. Then he turned the card over and read a statement about the purpose and value of the competition. I guess it was part of the thick packet of rules he'd complained about. There was nothing on the card about the contest helping identify potential members of an evil organization. But then again, I wasn't expecting anything like that.

After he'd finished with the card, Principal Ambrose said, "There will be three sections to the competition— athletic, academic, and creative."

I noticed that Abigail was staring at the bleachers. All the kids we knew were there. Not just our friends like Adam and Denali, but lots of other kids, like Shawna and the rest of the popular crowd. Some of those kids were the mean ones who already liked to make fun of Abigail. In a minute or two, they were going to find out how smart she was.

"I think your life is about to change," I said.

"I think it will be good for me." She held out her hand, palm down. "So let's do it."

I put my hand on top of hers. Mookie put his hand

on top of mine. "Team Mookie!" he shouted as we raised our hands high.

"All right," Principal Ambrose said. "Let's get this over with. Good luck to all of you. May the best team win. Quickly, if possible."

Rodney smirked at me. Mort settled back in his seat. Eddy grinned like he was about to get into a stomping match with a cricket. He had no idea what he was up against. If Abigail was a cricket, Eddy was a flea. I hid my own grin.

Ms. Delambre grabbed some file cards from her purse, and got another set from Ms. Otranto. She shuffled them, then said, "We're going to start with a series of questions. Hit your buzzer when you know the answer. A correct response earns ten points. Be careful—there will be a ten-point penalty for each incorrect answer. In that case, the other team will be given a chance to provide the correct answer without any risk of a penalty."

We put our hands over the buzzers. "Our first subject is famous people. Ready?" Ms. Delambre asked.

We all nodded.

"This author, who was born in Mumbai back when it was called Bombay—"

Buzzzzz!!!!

Abigail hit her buzzer.

Principal Ambrose glared at her, but she ignored him and said, "Rudyard Kipling."

Ms. Delambre looked like she'd been whacked on

the head. She stared at the card for a moment, then said, "Yes. You're right. Rudyard Kipling, author of *The Jungle Book* and other beloved stories. Very good. Ten points for your team."

"Had to be," Abigail whispered to me. "They aren't going to ask us stuff we don't know, so the answer couldn't possibly be an author kids aren't familiar with, like Salman Rushdie or Frederic William Farrar. Right?"

"Yeahhhhh . . . right . . ." I was just happy she knew the answer.

"Our next subject is famous mathematical formulas." Ms. Delambre said. "Here's the question: What—?"

Buzzzzz!!!!

"The Pythagorean theorem," Abigail said.

The card fell from Ms. Delambre's hand.

Abigail shrugged. "Well, it's the only famous math formula you'd expect kids our age to have possibly heard of, so there was no point waiting for the rest of the question."

"Uh, that's the correct answer. Another ten points for your team. The next subject is astronomy. This densest—"

Buzzzzz!!!!!

"Black hole," Abigail said. "Also known as a neutron star."

And so it went. Mort didn't seem too upset, but Rodney and Eddy glared at us the whole time. As our score grew, so did the temperature of the death rays shooting from their eyes. The audience, which had been a bit twitchy at first, grew silent. Twice, Eddy buzzed in before Abigail, but he made wild guesses and lost points.

We finished the academic round leading Rodney's team by a score of 200 to minus-20.

Next, it was time for the athletic part.

"I think your secret is definitely out," I said to Abigail. I glanced at the audience. There were still enough open mouths spread around the bleachers to make the room very dangerous for flies. While I felt bad that she'd revealed a secret she wanted to keep, it was nice to have someone else get stared at. "You could have held back a little," I said.

"What's the point?" she said. "If I'm going to reveal the truth, I might as well make it the entire truth. It's better to be a superfreak than an ordinary one. And you're right—we need the points."

"I held back," Mookie said. "Just think of me as our secret weapon. If Abigail needed help, I would have jumped right in."

"Good strategy," I said.

Mr. Lomux walked over to the microphone. I think he was the only person in the gym who didn't seem to understand how amazing Abigail's performance was. "We're going to test you for speed, strength, and endurance," he said.

Well, I was good at one of those. I had plenty of endurance. My muscles never got tired. Abigail had explained it to me a while ago. It had something to do with the way chemicals build up in muscles when we exercise.

So we were in good shape for endurance. But we were in a little trouble for speed and a lot for strength. Mort was fast, and Rodney was strong. I hoped it wouldn't matter.

The speed part was first. It was a shuttle run. We had to pick one member to compete. "I'll do it," Mookie said.

He put up a good effort, but Mort blew him away. I wasn't surprised. Mort's a good athlete.

"Hey, second place isn't bad," Mookie said when he came back to our table. "That would be silver in the Olympics."

"Yeah, you did great," I said.

Endurance was easy. We had to see who could climb up and down the ropes the most times without stopping. I totally beat Mort at that. After it was clear I'd won, I went up and down three more times, to add points to our total score, and then pretended I was too tired to keep going. I didn't want anyone to get suspicious. But it wasn't totally unbelievable that a skinny kid like me would be good at rope climbing.

"Now for strength." Mr. Lomux reached into a bag and pulled out some boxing gloves. Rodney raced over and grabbed a pair. He didn't seem surprised at the plan.

"That's not strength," I said.

"It is if I say it is," Mr. Lomux said. "So, who wants to take a beating for your side?"

"Nobody," I said. "We're way ahead on points. We've already locked in a win." Our huge lead in the first part, plus my win on the ropes, put us too far ahead for them to catch us, even if they won the boxing and the creative part.

Mr. Lomux shook his head and gave me the sort of smile I hadn't seen since I'd visited the shark tank at the aquarium. "According to the rules, a team has to compete in every event. If you drop out, you lose. So, who's boxing for your team?"

"I'll do it," I said. It looked like I was going to get a chance to test out my rock-hard bones.

7

Head Bangers

Mr. Lomux had put down tape on the floor at one end of the gym to mark out a boxing ring.

"This is going to be awesome," Mookie said as he laced on my gloves.

"It's definitely going to be quick," I said. Either I'd deck Rodney right away, or he'd clobber me. This wasn't going to be some sort of ten-round dance like you see on TV. It would be more like a video game where each player had nothing but finishing moves. I just hoped Rodney didn't rip my spine out of my body and beat me on the head with it.

Over at his table, Rodney pounded his gloves together and grinned at me. He still hadn't learned. But I guess I'd never actually beaten him face-to-face. The last time we'd battled, I'd taken him out in the dark, and he never really knew what had happened. This time, if I beat him, there'd be no doubt I was responsible. And no doubt he'd be hungry for revenge.

Mr. Lomux called both of us into the taped area, then stepped between us. He held up his stopwatch. "There'll be three two-minute rounds."

"No, there won't." Rodney smacked his gloves together again. "There'll be five seconds of pain."

"Keep it clean." Mr. Lomux winked at Rodney. Great. He was probably hoping Rodney would pull some sort of dirty trick.

"Box!" Mr. Lomux said. He clicked his stopwatch and backed up a step. He didn't move too far. I guess he wanted to see my destruction from up close.

Rodney rushed at me. He raised his right fist like he was going to smack me in the head. I put my gloves up to block. But Rodney wasn't aiming for my head. He swung his fist back and around in a big loop, like a softball pitcher windmilling the ball. He came in low. Real low. He hit me below the belt, hard enough to nearly lift me off my feet.

"Oops," he said, like it was an accident. But he couldn't help grinning. I knew he'd done it on purpose. He stood there, waiting. I guess he expected me to go down. That's what should have happened. If a guy gets hit below the belt, he drops, curls up, and waits for the sickening waves of pain to go away. I caught a soccer ball down there once, and it hadn't been fun.

But I don't feel pain. And Rodney had given me an opening. I dropped my arms down like I was about to crumple. I bent so low, my gloves touched the gym floor. Then I exploded, leaping up and swinging a hard right from halfway across the planet, catching Rodney on the side of his jaw. I guess the padding in the gloves wasn't enough to cushion my hardened bones. Rodney went flying so fast, I threw a second punch at where he'd been before it sank in on me that he wasn't there anymore.

As I was missing Rodney's jaw with my left, I heard a sickening crack, like someone had slammed a gigantic walnut with an enormous sledgehammer. I'd knocked Rodney right into Mr. Lomux. Their heads smacked together. The both went down.

Rodney moaned. That was good. I'm glad he wasn't knocked totally out. But it was obvious he wasn't ready for more. I guess he could add boxing to the list of sports he was going to have nightmares about.

Mr. Lomux shook his head hard and staggered to his feet. He looked like he wasn't quite sure where he was. After a moment, he grabbed my wrist and raised my arm in the air. The side of his face had started to swell up and turn purple. "Winner," he said. Then he wandered off toward his office. He walked into the wall next to the door twice before he made it through the opening.

I heard another moan. Rodney got up, wobbled over to his team, and took a seat. Then he put his head down on the table and started snoring.

"Well," Principal Ambrose said as he grabbed his coat, "it looks like we're done." He pointed at our table. "They win. Thank you all for coming. Have a great weekend."

He headed for the door.

"Hey—there's still one part left!" Eddy yelled after him. He pushed Rodney's shoulder. "Wake up. We need you."

Rodney lifted his head a couple of inches. A thin strand of drool stretched from his mouth to the table. "Five more minutes, Mom. Please." He dropped his head back down with a gentle thud and started snoring again.

And that was it. We'd won. I glanced toward the bleachers. Everyone was staring at us. I didn't like that, but there was nothing I could do about it.

"I hate to say it, but I'm starting to feel sorry for Rodney," Mookie said when I got back to our table. "It's like his whole life is some sort of Whac-A-Mole game, except there's only one hole, and he keeps sticking his head out."

I held up my gloves so he could unlace them. "Yeah, I guess I kind of feel a little sorry for him, too. But I'm sure he'll do something to change that."

"Ewww," Mookie said. "That doesn't look very pretty."

I stared at my hand. "Yeah, you're right." It was sort of squished. The bone might have been really hard, but

I guess my skin and muscles weren't in very good shape. I pushed my hand around with my other fingers and got it looking sort of normal. Maybe superstrong bones weren't all that great when they were covered with rotting flesh.

"That's not the only thing that looks nasty," Abigail said. She pointed toward the other table. Eddy glared at us like we'd just stolen his bicycle right out from under him. Rodney might have been knocked off his feet, but Eddy was knocked off his throne as the smartest kid in the school. He definitely wasn't happy about that.

Mort got up from the other table, walked over, and held out his hand. "Good job," he said. "Your team deserved to win."

"Hey, you kicked our butt in the shuttle run," I said as I shook hands with him. I noticed my hand was a little squished again. I'd have to try to avoid getting congratulated about anything.

"Yeah. I did okay. But I wouldn't want to match brains with little Einstein, here." Mort grinned at Abigail, then walked away.

"That wasn't so bad," I said to Abigail. "This isn't kindergarten. Nobody is going to tease you for being smart."

"We'll see. Mort's just one kid. I have a whole class to deal with." Then she smiled and said, "Little Einstein . . . That's kind of nice."

A bunch of other kids came over to congratulate us.

Most of them gave me a strange look, like they weren't sure it was safe to go near me.

Mookie pointed to his shirt as we left the table. "Score one for Team Mookie. I think snagging second place in the shuttle run locked up the victory for us. It might look like a simple event, but it takes real strategy. The secret is in the turns."

He pivoted on his heels a couple of times, then stumbled and fell flat on his face. "Hey, look—I'm doing a Rodney imitation."

My parents came up to me on the way out. "That was very impressive," Dad said. "Where'd you learn to box?"

"Video games," I said. "I play a lot at my friends' houses. I'd play at home if I had my own system."

Dad ignored the hint.

"I was afraid you'd hurt that poor boy," Mom said.

"Rodney's tough," I said.

"When did you decide to enter this contest?" Dad asked.

I shrugged. "The other day. It was a last-minute thing. But I guess we're going to the second round. That's okay with you, right? It's just over in Hurston Lakes. But if we win that one, I think the third round is going to be in Princeton."

Mom and Dad both nodded. Good. It looked like we were all set.

"Mr. Murphy will be happy we won," Mookie said after my parents left. "You should send him a message."

"He already knows," I said.

"How?" Mookie looked up at the ceiling. "Did he plant a camera or something?"

"Nope. He was there."

"I didn't see him," Mookie said.

"The old man in the second row," I said. "The one with the cane. That was him."

"Really?" Mookie glanced back over his shoulders at the empty bleachers. "How do you know?"

"You can't hide those ears," I said. "Even under a fuzzy wig. And he was the only person in the audience who didn't seem surprised by Abigail's intelligence." I turned to Abigail. "Speaking of hiding—how did it feel not hiding your brain power?"

"Nice," she said. "I could get used to this. Hey, you guys want to come over and celebrate?"

"Sure." That sounded good to me. I was proud of our team. But when we got to Abigail's house, we found a big surprise waiting for her, and that surprise had brought an even bigger surprise, especially for me.

8

Guess Who's Not Coming to Dinner

That's weird," **Abigail** said when we reached her house. "All the curtains are drawn. I hope everything's okay."

I saw what she meant. There was a big window in the front of the house. Usually, you could see inside. But the curtains were closed. Mr. Murphy had taught me that it was important to pay attention to anything around you that suddenly changed.

"Mom?" Abigail called when we went inside. "Where are you?"

"In the kitchen," her mom called back. "Are you alone?"

"Nathan and Mookie are with me," Abigail said.

"What's going on?" I asked.

Abigail shrugged. "No idea." She took two steps, then stopped and said, "Wait. There's only one explanation. Ohmygosh!" She raced down the hall and disappeared into the kitchen.

"Twinkle!" someone shouted.

It can't be.

"Uncle Zardo!" Abigail said.

It is.

"It's him," I said to Mookie. "Nobody else calls her Twinkle."

"Not unless they want a kick in the shins. But I thought he was hiding out on some island," Mookie said.

"Yeah, he was on Bezimo Island. It's in the Caribbean. I guess he came back." I went to the kitchen. Abigail's uncle Zardo, the crazy scientist who'd made the formula that killed me, was sitting on a stool by the kitchen counter. He looked different. He had a tan, his dark hair was dyed blond, and he'd shaved his mustache. But he still had eyes that seemed to be seeing a different world from the one the rest of us saw. At the moment, Abigail was giving him a hug.

"Nathan," she said, turning her head toward me, "look who's here."

"I see." I scanned the table to make sure there weren't any bottles of chemicals, or anything else that could make things even worse for me. "Aren't the police after you?"

"They have more important things to do," Zardo said. "That whole incident at the college was just a small misunderstanding. Nothing worth worrying about. I'm sure they've forgotten all about me."

"Then why are the curtains closed?" I asked.

"I'd rather not remind them of our encounter. I might have neglected to ask their permission before I slipped away." He turned to Abigail's mom. "Do you have any of that bread I like? The type with the thick crust? I haven't had a decent grilled cheese sandwich since I left the country."

"I'm all out," Abigail's mom said. "I'll run to the store. It won't take long. It's just two blocks away."

As soon as the front door closed, Abigail's uncle leaned toward me and said, "Let me tell you why I'm here. When I heard what the Hurt-Be-Gone did to you, I started doing research. Luckily, I was already in the perfect place. Bezimo Island is the source of some of the most believable of the original zombie legends, as well as being the only place on earth where the corpse flower grows naturally. I felt that if a cure existed, I'd find it there."

"A cure?" I still hoped I'd get to be alive again some day, but I guess part of me had accepted that it might never happen. I was trying to make the best of a dead situation.

"Yes. A cure. I believe I've found one."

I didn't leap up in the air and shout. Zardo's first

formula, which was supposed to erase bad feelings, had wiped out my body's feelings instead, and slowly turned me from a living kid to a half-dead zombie. It was actually a formula Abigail had created, but her uncle had used the corpse flower by mistake instead of the corpus flower. There was no reason to believe anything he came up with would work. I looked at Abigail.

"What's the cure?" she asked him.

"Didn't you get my text messages?" he asked.

"That was you?" Abigail grabbed her phone and pulled up her old messages. "What in the world does *hunting cur morel eater* mean? Or *rarf lower?*"

Zardo stared at the phone for a moment. "Oh, dear. That was supposed to be *Hunting cure. More Later.* And, of course, *Rare flower.* I guess my texteaser needs tweaking."

"Texteaser?" Abigail asked.

He reached in his pocket and pulled out some sort of mechanical box with ten metal thumbs on it. He slid a phone into a slot under the thumbs, then shoved two fingers into an opening in the bottom. The thumbs started wriggling, tapping the surface of the box. "You can do everything with a pair of fingers. It makes texting so much easier. Especially for people who are on the move a lot. At least, it will when I iron out a few wrinkles."

I had a feeling we could get way off track if I didn't stop them. "The cure?" I asked.

"The corpse flower caused the problem," he said. "According to legend, there's an anima flower than can bring someone halfway back to life. Since you're only halfway dead, that should be enough to do the trick."

"So that's what *enima flow* was supposed to be. Anima flower. Is it on Bezimo Island?" Abigail asked.

"No. I'm fairly certain it has to be on the opposite side of the world," Zardo said. "You have to admit, that sort of makes sense."

Abigail glanced up at the ceiling for a second. I guess it didn't take her long to figure out a simple geography problem—simple for her, at least.

"Somewhere near the Philippines," she said.

"That's what I believe." He handed her a sheet of paper. "These are the other ingredients, and the steps required to mix everything. The rest should be easy to get. The flower will require a bit of travel."

"We can't go there," Abigail said.

"But I can," Uncle Zardo said. "I just wanted to see you before I went there, and let you know I'm trying to fix things."

"That's sweet," Abigail said.

"And borrow a bit of money from your mother for the trip," he added.

"That's typical." She gave him another hug. "I missed you."

"I missed you, too, Twinkle."

I guess the second *Twinkle* was too much for Mookie. He struggled hard, but he failed to hold back his snicker.

He stopped laughing as soon as Abigail kicked his shin. That turned his snicker into a howl.

An instant later, his howl had company. I heard a siren somewhere off in the distance. My hearing is better than anyone who's alive because I don't have the sound of blood rushing through my head. "You sure nobody knows you're in the country?" I asked Zardo.

He frowned, looked toward the window as the siren grew louder, then said, "Why take chances? I better get going. It's a long way to the Philippines." He hopped off his stool and dashed out the back door.

The siren got even louder, then shot past the house. I watched through the window as an ambulance streaked by. "Not the police," I said.

"Not this time," Abigail said. "But they'd track him down sooner or later if he stayed around. Uncle Zardo is sort of like a magnet for trouble. It's probably a good idea for him to keep moving."

"Do you really think he found a cure?" I asked. "He's not exactly the best scientist on the planet."

"It's possible. I'll try to do some research on the anima flower tonight," Abigail said. "Knowing him, it probably has some other effects he thinks he can use to get rich. But that doesn't mean it can't help you."

The front door opened. Abigail's mom came back in, carrying a small bag of groceries. When she reached the kitchen, she looked at the empty stool. "Where's Zardo?"

"He had to get going," Abigail said.

"But you're still making grilled cheese, right?" Mookie asked.

I wanted to believe Abigail's uncle was going somewhere that would help me. I wasn't letting my hopes get too high. Right now, I needed to keep my attention on winning the next round of Brainy Brawny. It wouldn't be as easy as beating Rodney, Eddy, and Mort. There'd be teams there from all over South Jersey.

"Aren't you worried about him?" Mookie asked.

"No," Abigail said. "I'm worried about school on Monday."

So was I. Now that I had some time to think about our victory in the gym, I realized it was going to change the way kids treated me. Whether it would be a good or bad change, I couldn't guess.

9

Slipping Pasta Security

Saturday night, as I was lying in bed, my radio switched on by itself. I went over to shut it off, but a message popped up in the little window where you see the station number. Words scrolled across the panel: GO TO BUM. I saw a small wisp of smoke drift from the back of the radio. I unplugged it from the wall before it could burst into flames.

After I was sure my parents were in bed, I snuck out of the house and went to the Museum of Tile and Grout.

Once I reached BUM, Mr. Murphy said, "That was an impressive display of boxing skill, Nathan. It was clever how you used his actions to lower his defense. You can definitely think on your feet." He let out a little laugh. "Or should I say, on your toes? Perhaps I really should look into some martial arts training for you."

"I'd love that." I threw a kick, and then a karate chop.

"But not this evening," he said.

"Am I doing some spy training?" I asked. Mr. Murphy had taught me all sorts of spycraft, both at BUM head-quarters and out in the world. I knew how to follow people, and how to make a drop. I'd even learned a bit about secret codes, though that wasn't my best thing.

"Not tonight. We have a mission," he said. "It should be an easy one, but I assure you, it is vital."

"What is it?"

Mr. Murphy looked away.

"You're not going to tell me, are you?"

He shook his head. "No, I'm absolutely going to tell you. I was just figuring out how to tell you."

I waited.

"We uncovered a laboratory that is doing botanical research," he said. "It's funded by people who help support RABID. We believe they're growing the corpse flower, along with a variety of other rare and dangerous plants."

"And you want the place destroyed?" I asked.

"That's the mission."

"So why were you worried about telling me?" I asked.

"The greatest danger for any spy occurs when he is personally involved with a mission. If you start thinking about the corpse flower, and what it did to you, you might get distracted, or make a foolish decision. Can you handle this mission?"

"For sure."

"Are you ready?"

"Always."

We took a regular elevator down to another floor. The door opened into a large room. Mr. Murphy went over to a table and picked up a package wrapped in plastic. "Here. Take this."

"What is it?"

"Clothes," he said. "You really don't want to walk around covered in sauce."

"Sauce?"

"Spaghetti sauce," he said. "You're infiltrating the facility by hiding inside a drum of spaghetti sauce."

"You're kidding." I checked his face for any sign of a smile.

"Not at all. It's the only way we've come up with to get an agent inside. Security there is very tight."

I took the package. Then I pointed to my shirt. "What about the clothes I'm wearing?"

"You might want to leave them here," he said.

Great. I seemed to end up in my underwear a lot more than you'd think a superspy would. I took off my pants and shirt. I could see myself climbing out of the drum, dripping sauce from every part of me. "What about my body? That's going to be soaked."

"There should be a sink or something over there," Mr. Murphy said. "You'll be in an area where food is prepared. I'm sure a resourceful spy such as yourself will have no trouble finding a way to clean up."

"What do I do when I get there?"

Mr. Murphy handed me a small package wrapped in plastic. "First, you'll unscrew the lid of the drum. After you get cleaned up, find the room with the corpse flower. Unwrap the package. There's a small device in here with a power cord. Plug it into any wall outlet."

I took the package from him. It was small but heavy. "It won't explode, will it?"

"I certainly hope it will."

"What?" I almost dropped the package.

"Relax. I'm kidding. RABID blows things up. We don't. This will just cause the wiring in the whole building to slowly overheat. People will have plenty of time to escape. Nobody will be harmed, but the plants growing in the lab will be destroyed. Many of them could be used for dangerous purposes. After you've installed the device, go back to the kitchen. Somewhere along the rear wall, there'll be a chute."

"What kind of chute?" I asked.

"It's a garbage chute," he said.

"Great, you're sending me into a pile of garbage again."

Mr. Murphy shook his head. "Not this time. The chute empties directly into a river."

"A river?" I wasn't sure whether I was more annoyed that garbage was getting dumped into a river, or that I was getting dumped into one.

"What can I say? They're not very nice people. But that isn't important. Listen carefully. When you hit the water, stay under and keep swimming. Don't come to the surface until you reach the other bank. I'll be waiting for you up there. Questions?"

"Does it have to be spaghetti sauce?"

"Would you prefer borscht?"

"What's that?"

"Beet soup."

"I guess not. Let's do it." I tucked the package under my arm and walked over to the drum. There was a chair next to it for me to stand on.

"In you go," Mr. Murphy said. "After we screw on the lid, you'll be loaded on a truck. Then there will be a short plane ride. After that—"

"A plane ride? I can't go that far away." Tomorrow was Sunday, so I didn't have to be up early for school, but my parents would check on me sooner or later if I didn't show up for lunch.

"You'll be back home in plenty of time," Mr. Murphy said. "It's an extremely fast plane. Once you land, you'll be loaded onto another truck, and then the drum will be brought inside the target facility. Once the drum stops moving, count to one thousand before you come out. We don't want the delivery men to spot you."

I stepped into the sauce. It rose up as I sank down. "Are you sure I'll be home in time?"

"Absolutely. Good luck. Oh—one more thing. Stay alert. There might be armed guards."

I scrunched down and let the sauce cover my head. It was strange. I could feel the weight of it. Not in a big way. It wasn't like I was being crushed. But I could tell that I was in something a lot thicker than water. Or milk. I couldn't help laughing. Milk. Sauce. I was working my way through a balanced meal. Maybe I could hide in a crate of artichokes next.

A moment later, I felt the drum rising. The noise from outside was muffled by the sauce, but it sounded like they were using a forklift.

Here I go.

It all went as Mr. Murphy said. I could feel the truck moving for a while. Finally, it stopped. I heard the truck door open. I started moving again.

Whoa!

Even though I couldn't see anything, I could tell I was going fast. My body was pressed hard against the side of the drum. I couldn't guess how long I was in the air. After we landed, I felt the drum getting moved to a second truck. That ride was a lot bouncier. Finally, I had another forklift ride. Then all the motion stopped.

After I counted to one thousand, I unscrewed the top of the drum. There were handles inside that made it easy. When I climbed out, I saw I was in some sort of storage area in the back of a large kitchen. I found a sink and managed to wash off the sauce, and then dry myself with dish towels. I wiped up the floor and put the lid back on the drum, just in case any guards passed through while I was on my mission. After I got dressed, I went out to look for the plants.

I was in some sort of building with several labs on each floor. I guess they had a kitchen so people could cook meals for the workers. I saw several signs, but they weren't in English. I found the plant-growth area in a huge room halfway down a hall on the first floor.

As I was walking into the room, I heard voices behind me.

10

Back in a flash

I ducked down behind a large carton and waited as two guards came down the hall and went through the room. I wasn't worried. One of the advantages of being dead is that people never sense that I'm around. I could stare right at the guards, and they'd never get that twitchy feeling of being watched.

But only one of them was a guard. He was in some sort of uniform. The other was dressed in a lab coat. They were both wearing gas masks strapped around their heads, so I could only see a little bit of their faces. The guy in the suit was bald, with a fat neck. Even through the gas mask, I could see he had beady little eyes that reminded me of an evil cartoon snake. The guard had a crew cut. His eyes didn't remind me of anything.

The bald guy pointed to a glass case and said something in another language. There was a plant inside the case. The guard opened the case and took out the plant. I guess it was poisonous. It's a good thing BUM had sent me on the mission, and not someone who'd be hurt by poison.

As they left, I glared at the guy in the lab coat. He was probably the one who'd given RABID the corpse flower. Maybe I could sneak up behind them and rip off his gas mask. That would teach him a lesson.

But it would also get me caught and ruin the mission. I'd have to settle for destroying his plants. I unwrapped the device. It looked like the kind of power supply that comes with a laptop computer or a video game system, but bigger. I needed to do one thing before I plugged it in.

I scanned the tables. I didn't have any trouble finding it.

It was small and dull, like a dead piece of meat.

"So this is it . . . ," I said. The corpse flower. It didn't look like much. Abigail had told me there were actually two other plants also called corpse flowers. But they weren't as rare, and they couldn't help turn someone into a zombie.

There were other flowers in the room. Some of them looked pretty dangerous. A couple had spikes or sharp needles. There was even some agony vera. I remembered it from the encyclopedia article. Weird. I hadn't expected to ever run into it. But now that I had, I figured I'd keep seeing it all over the place.

The plants weren't all ugly. One flower, with silver petals, almost seemed to glow. I thought about bringing that one home for my mom. But she wasn't really good at watering plants. It was kinder to have it die quickly here than slowly in our family room. I reached out and touched it. The blossom withered beneath my fingers, like it had been scorched. I guess Mom wasn't the worst plant killer in the family.

I plugged in the device and watched it for a moment. I couldn't see anything, but I heard a quiet hum, like in the power supply from Dad's old train set. It was working. I'd done my job. I headed back to the storage room by the kitchen.

Sure enough, there was a large chute on the back wall. I lifted the door and crawled inside. The instant I'd slipped in as far as my waist, I found myself plunging through some sort of tube. A moment later, I shot out of the chute right above a river. I hit the water at an angle and let myself go down. The current wasn't bad. I started swimming. The bank wasn't all that far, but I don't think anyone who needed to breathe could have made it.

I got out and looked back. I could see a building across the river. There were guards on the roof. I guess that's why Mr. Murphy had told me to stay under the water until I reached the other side.

I climbed the bank and found myself next to a road. Mr. Murphy was just fifty yards away, standing by a car.

"All done?" he asked when I reached him.

"All done."

"Excellent."

"Hey, wait! It's morning!" I spun around as it hit me that it wasn't dark outside. The sun was above the horizon. I'd never get home in time. Mom would be totally panicked when she didn't find me in my bed. She'd probably already called the police. I was going to get grounded for life—which I guess meant forever.

"Relax," Mr. Murphy said. "The sun isn't rising. It's setting."

"What!" That was even worse.

Mr. Murphy laughed. "We're rather far from New Jersey. It's still dark back home."

"Are you sure?"

"See for yourself." He held up his watch. According to the dial, it was three thirty in the morning. I guess he left it on eastern time.

Instead of going anywhere, he sat down on the bank and handed me a pair of binoculars. "We have plenty of time. You should observe the results of your efforts."

I watched the building. Nothing happened for a couple of minutes. Then I noticed the guards on the roof start scurrying around, like there was an emergency but they weren't sure what to do about it. I saw several of them talking on two-way radios. I scanned the rest of the building and saw more guards running out the door. The guards on the roof climbed down a ladder. There was a bit of a glow behind several of the windows.

"I think things are heating up," I said.

"I think so. We'd better get going. Our transport should be arriving very soon."

We drove down the road, ending up at a landing strip. It wasn't even an airport—just a cleared area. Something had already landed. Something awesome.

"We're going in that?"

"Yes."

"Cool. Will it explode?"

"Hardly. It isn't from BUM. We're getting a ride from the air force. And you're persistently annoying."

"That's just one of my many useful skills." I turned my attention back to our ride. It was some sort of jet. I'd never seen one like it before, but I had a feeling it might not be something the air force told people about. It was very flat and very black. It wouldn't have been out of place launching from the belly of a spaceship.

"So, any time you want a jet, you just ask for it? That's awesome." I wondered what Mookie would think about that.

"Not when I want one," Mr. Murphy said. "When I *need* one. And, yes, BUM has total instant access to whatever transportation we need. If necessary, I could have us cruising off the coast in a nuclear submarine on a moment's notice."

We took our seats behind the pilot. He handed me an oxygen mask. I was about to tell him I didn't need one, when Mr. Murphy said, "Thank you," and slipped it over my head.

Mr. Murphy didn't say anything, but I could read the words in his stare. *Nobody needs to know you don't breathe.* Right. There was no reason to let the pilot know my secret. All he needed to know was that he was taking us somewhere.

And he took us somewhere, for sure. Fast. Superfast. When we left the landing strip, the jet didn't take off. It took *up*. Straight up. Then it shot forward.

When we landed, Mr. Murphy led me to another car. "Any chance you could get Mookie a jet ride?" I asked.

He snorted, but didn't even bother to answer. After we got in the car, he said, "Fix your face."

"What are you talking about?"

He flipped down my sun visor and pointed to the mirror on the back of it. "You look like one of those ancient Hollywood stars who's had too much plastic surgery."

I checked out my reflection. Yeesh. I guess the g-forces from flying had smushed my skin toward my ears. I put my hands on the sides of my face and moved everything back to where it belonged.

"Better?" I asked.

"Definitely. Though your plasticity might come in handy. You could become a master of disguise. Or disgust."

He cackled way too loudly at his own joke and almost missed the next turn.

I pushed gently against my nose. It moved to the side. I straightened it, sat back, and tried not to think about how I was slowly turning into a pile of gooey flesh wrapped around strong bones. The Play-Doh kid. Yeah, that would be just wonderful.

Mr. Murphy drove pretty fast again. After a while, I started recognizing the roads. He was driving me home.

I settled back in my seat. "That was a very cool jet."

"Yes, it was. There are some advantages to being a spy."

Since he was sharing information, I figured I'd ask the one thing I'd been wondering about since he'd first recruited me. "When will I meet other agents?"

"You've met some of us," Mr. Murphy said.

"No. I mean agents like me. Other kids who've had useful misadventures."

"When you need to," Mr. Murphy said. "Right now, there's no need."

"But we're sort of in the same club," I said. "It would be nice to get together."

"Nathan, this isn't a social activity. I didn't recruit you so you could find someone to play checkers with or trade baseball cards. We're fighting the bad guys."

"I don't see how it would hurt," I said.

"Forget it. That's not happening until there's a reason

for it. Look how much trouble we had the last time I didn't follow proper procedures."

I let it drop. I could sort of understand what he was talking about. Thanks to one little slip, he'd been kidnapped by RABID last winter, and beaten up pretty badly. That could have turned out a lot worse. Still, I thought it would be good to meet kids who'd been doing this for longer than I had. They could probably give me some useful tips. And maybe some new ways to annoy Mr. Murphy. I guess that would have to wait.

I got home just before sunrise. Right now, my insomnia—or, as Mookie liked to call it, my *inzomnia*—didn't bother me at all.

There were plenty of times when I wished I could sleep. It was one of the things I missed about being alive. But if I needed sleep, I'd probably feel exhausted after staying up all night carrying out the mission. I'd be too tired to enjoy the feeling of success. So tonight, inzomnia was a good thing. It helped me be a spy.

Sunday afternoon, I met up with my friends at Abigail's place.

"I haven't found a single thing about the anima flower on the Internet," Abigail said.

"That's not good. So it isn't real?" I was glad I hadn't gotten my hopes up about a cure.

"I didn't say that. Not everything is on the Internet. There are some books I can check. There are all sorts of old newspapers and magazines that aren't on the Internet."

"Then how can you search them?" I asked.

"They have indexes," Abigail said.

"On the Internet?" Mookie asked.

"No, in other books," Abigail said. "People did re-search before there was an Internet. And even before there were any computers at all. They looked things up. They found information. It will be fun. I'll go to the county library after school tomorrow."

"I'm still searching for a cure, too," Mookie said. "I'll bet I come up with one first." He stared up at the ceiling, the way Abigail always does when she's thinking. A moment later, he said, "I got it! This is perfect!"

"What?" I asked.

"We've been looking at it wrong the whole time." He threw a smirk in Abigail's direction.

"I can't wait to hear this," she said.

"Forget that stupid flower. All we have to do is find a vampire and get him to bite you," Mookie said. "Then you'll never die."

"I'm already dead," I said.

"But you won't get deader," Mookie said. "See? It's perfect. No rotting or anything."

"Except, there aren't any vampires," Abigail said.

Mookie tossed her a second smirk. "Just like there aren't any zombies?"

"It's not the same thing," Abigail said.

"Of course not," Mookie said. "One's a vampire and one's a zombie."

"Great," Abigail said. "You look for vampires. I'll keep looking for the anima flower."

11

That Smarts

Rodney was waiting for me in front of the school Monday morning, when I went to meet up with my friends. I clenched my fists, just in case, but kept my hands at my sides. If I had to defend myself, I figured I could do even more damage without a boxing glove. But even Rodney wasn't stupid enough to start something on school property.

"That was a lucky punch," he said. He poked my shoulder and glared.

"Yeah, I felt pretty lucky," I said. That was true. I was lucky my bones had been hardened, and I was lucky I'd been able to catch Rodney by surprise while he was waiting for me to crumple from the low punch.

"There's something wrong with you," he said. "You're not a normal kid."

I shrugged. "I've been hearing that for years."

He threw a punch at my head, but stopped short. "You didn't even blink."

"I've got nerves of steel," I said.

"Whatever's going on, I'm gonna figure it out," he said. "And then they'll make us the winners. You cheated. There's no way you could ever beat me for real. You're just a big lousy cheater."

He walked off. I watched him go join Eddy. That worried me. Rodney wasn't smart enough to figure anything out by himself. But even though Eddy was nowhere near as smart as Abigail, he still might be able to put things together.

"Wow," Mookie said. "Rodney really lives in his own little universe. I guess it's a Rodneyverse."

"He can't imagine anyone ever beating him at anything," Abigail said. "That's typical for a bully. So to him, he just can't admit you actually won the boxing match fairly. He has to believe you cheated."

"I guess if you think about what happened, I really did sort of cheat. But not the way he thinks." I pulled my shirt collar away from my neck and looked at my shoulder. There was a small dent where Rodney had poked me.

"And he cheated, too," Mookie said, "trying to hit you below the belt. That was pretty slimy."

"He did more than try," I said. "I wasn't standing on my toes because I wanted to be a ballet dancer. But I'll bet he can convince himself it was okay to do that." I put my thumb on one side of the dent and my first finger on the other, then stretched my skin until the dent popped out.

"Absolutely," Abigail said. "A famous philosopher once said, 'No one does wrong willingly.'"

"He'd never met Rodney," Mookie said. "Or Mr. Lomux. Hey, speaking about doing wrong, look who's coming over."

"Now what?" I watched Shawna cross the school lawn. She'd been mean to each of us at some point during the year. But she'd gotten a bit nicer after her horrible experience at the Halloween party, when I'd slipped my snapped-off finger into her glass of orange soda. I know it was a terrible thing to do to, but I'd had no choice.

Abigail's words echoed back through my brain: *No one does wrong willingly.* I guess all of us can find an excuse for just about anything. Maybe that's why there were groups like RABID out there. They felt they were doing the right thing.

Shawna opened up her math book and pointed to a page. "We're having a test this afternoon, and I totally don't get this. Do you understand it?"

"Nope. I guess you and I have something in common," Mookie said. "How do you like that?"

Shawna let out a little snort of frustration, then pushed the book closer to Abigail. "I was talking to her."

Abigail glanced at the page, and then at her watch. "There's probably enough time before the bell. It's not difficult if you break it up into small steps. Come on—I think I can help you out."

They walked over to a bench near the flagpole and sat down. Abigail pointed to something on the page and talked. Shawna shook her head. Abigail talked some more. Shawna shook her head again. Abigail talked even more. Shawna nodded. It was a slow nod, like she was trying to squeeze a hard rubber ball against her body with her chin. Then there was a pause, followed by a larger nod.

Abigail talked a bit more. Then she patted Shawna on the shoulder. Shawna closed her book and ran off. Abigail walked back to us. "Wow," I said. "I'll bet you can sit at the popular table at lunch."

"I'd rather eat my own liver—with anchovies and horseradish," Abigail said.

"I like horseradish," Mookie said. "Even if it does give me gas."

"Air gives you gas," Abigail said. "Water gives you gas. I think even sunlight gives you gas."

"So I might as well eat lots of horseradish," Mookie said.

"You were able to help her?" I asked.

"Yeah. I think she understands it now," Abigail said.

"How'd it feel?"

Abigail glanced back at the bench. "Nice." Just then, her purse beeped. She grabbed her phone. "It's from Uncle Zardo."

MAD TO COZY GIANT

"That's not telling us much," I said.

Abigail grinned. "What Uncle Zardo can scramble, I can unscramble. I wrote an app for my phone. It uses fuzzy logic to figure out what he was trying to send before the texteaser messed it up. Watch."

She pressed a button, and the message changed.

I MADE IT TO QASIGIANNGUIT

"Well, at least part of it is clear now," I said. "But I think your app needs work."

"My app is perfect. All of it is clear," Abigail said. "This is exactly what he wanted to text. Qasigiannguit is in Greenland."

"Greenland?" Mookie said. "Even I know that's not on the way to the Philippines from here. Or from anywhere."

Abigail shrugged. "Uncle Zardo doesn't always take the shortest route. There are some places he has to avoid."

"Like anywhere with police who are looking for him?" I asked.

"Sort of," Abigail said. "But don't worry. He'll get there."

The bell rang. Shawna and Rodney had just been the start of things. The day got even more interesting. When we walked into home base, Ms. Otranto smiled at Abigail and said, "Can I count on a little more class participation from this point onward?"

"Yes, ma'am," Abigail said.

All through class, every time Ms. Otranto asked a question, she looked directly at Abigail, even when she didn't raise her hand.

The same thing happened in science. Ms. Delambre gazed at Abigail like she wanted to adopt her. The whole time Ms. Delambre set up the experiment, she talked to Abigail. It was actually a pretty cool experiment. Ms. Delambre had hooked up a thermometer to a computer, and plugged that into a projector so the whole class could watch the display. We were going to see how much energy a lightbulb lost as heat.

It wasn't just the teachers who treated Abigail differently. The other kids looked at her like they expected her to answer everything. They looked at me, too, but in a different way. They were trying really hard to get me to like them. I got splattered with friendliness all morning.

"Hey, Nate, you were awesome in the gym."

"Want to come over after school? You can ride my dirt bike."

"Man, Nathan, I thought you were amazing on Saturday. Rodney looked like he'd been hit by a meteor."

"I got some cookies in my desk. Want one?"

They seemed to think that if I didn't like them, I'd hurt them. I wanted to scream at them, *Hey, I like you! I won't hurt you. I'm not a bully. Treat me like a normal kid!*

Except, of course, I wasn't a normal kid. And I had another secret that, if they knew it, would totally change the way they treated me. I was pretty sure nobody offers cookies to zombies or invites them over after school.

When it was time for recess, Mookie, Abigail, and I fled to the side of the school.

"I want to grab them and shake them," I said. "I want to tell them I won't hurt them." I turned toward the playground and shouted, "I won't hurt you! I'm not like Rodney."

"I just want them to stop staring," Abigail said. "But that'll happen. They won't stay amazed by us forever. Something else will distract them."

"I hope so." There was one other thing I was worried about. I checked my watch. Recess ended in about ten minutes. Right after the bell rang, I'd find out if an important part of my life had changed.

12

The Table Remains Stable

We went in for lunch. The classroom was one thing. You didn't really get to talk with your friends a whole lot in there. But lunch was something else: It was a social situation. Whoever you were in the lunchroom, that's who you were as a person. I noticed Abigail was walking very close to me.

"Careful. You're near death," I said.

"What?"

"I was trying to make a joke," I said.

"Oh. Yeah, I get it. Near death. Good one." She didn't laugh.

"Nervous?" I asked.

"A little. These are our friends. I don't want them to think we've been hiding important things from them."

"But we have," I said. "I have. You have. I'm still hiding something really big."

"I'm not hiding anything," Mookie said.

"In your case, there are some things you should keep to yourself," Abigail said.

We reached the table. Our group had once been the Second Besters—kids who weren't so good or bad at something that we stood out. I was the second-skinniest kid in class, Mookie was the second-fattest. Denali was the second-funniest. We were all second at something.

Abigail's original group, the Doomed, were the kids who'd been left without any group. They'd been stuck at their own table when school started, but they'd joined us earlier this year, after Mookie and I became friends with Abigail. So we were sort of a mixed group scooped up from the bottom of the ladder—or the bottom of the pool.

The instant I sat down, Ferdinand yelled, "Don't hit me!"

"Knock it off!" I shouted.

That was a mistake. Ferdinand squealed and dived under the table.

"He really should just keep his tray down there," Mookie said. He picked up Ferdinand's sandwich and handed it to him under the table.

That was true. Ferdinand spent a lot of time hiding.

I peeked under. "Hey, I only hit bullies. Okay?" I tried to keep my voice as gentle as possible.

Ferdinand nodded, but stayed where he was.

Meanwhile, Adam was staring at Abigail. "I guess I'm not a Second Bester," he said. He pointed across the cafeteria. "Eddy should be sitting at this table instead of me. He's the second-smartest kid in school."

"Nobody here likes Eddy," I said.

"Everybody here likes you," Abigail said. "You're part of the group."

"Everybody."

We all turned and looked. I think it was the first time any of us had heard Snail Girl say a word. She blushed and stared down at her tray.

"Then it would be smart of me to stay," Adam said. He picked up his peanut butter sandwich, sniffed it, then took a bite. He'd gotten into the habit of smelling all his food, ever since that unpleasant incident with the hamburger. I guess I couldn't blame him. He could blame me, but that's another story.

We all started eating. Everyone except for me, of course. And things, at least here at our lunch table, felt perfectly normal. Mookie stuffed his face and made gross comments. Denali made jokes. Adam and Abigail talked about things nobody else understood. Eventually, even Ferdinand climbed out and joined us.

"What do you think Mr. Lomux is going to do?" Mookie asked when we headed to gym.

"I don't know," I said. "But I bet it won't be fun."

Mr. Lomux obviously wanted to make me suffer. Luckily, he only seemed to know one way to do that— make me work out real hard. That, of course, didn't cause me any suffering at all. I could jog from here to California without stopping.

We ran laps for the first half of class. Then we started doing sit-ups and push-ups. I thought about acting exhausted and dropping out. But I was tired of him, and tired of how he pushed kids around. They really shouldn't let bullies become teachers.

I did everything he threw at us, and stuck with it even after most of the kids had dropped out. Maybe that was a mistake, because at the end of class, as I was walking out, he grabbed my shoulder and said, "There's something weird about you, Abercrombie."

"Just that I love gym," I said. "But I guess that's pretty weird."

I noticed that Eddy and Rodney hung back as everyone else was leaving. They huddled together with Mr. Lomux. I didn't like that, but there was nothing I could do about it.

13

Princeton Charming

It was weird having Dad drive us to Princeton for the regional finals. He was really proud of me for entering the Brainy Brawny competition. But I wasn't doing it for the reasons he thought. I guess if he knew the real reason, he'd be even prouder. He'd also totally stop me from doing it. Parents don't seem to want their kids to tackle evil organizations.

We'd had an easy win at the South Jersey round in Hurston Lakes. I figured things were about to get harder, but I wasn't worried. Abigail and I were wearing our new Belgosi Upper Elementary team shirts. Ms. Delambre had gotten them for us. Mookie had stuck with his Team Mookie shirt.

"I've dreamed of coming here," Abigail said as we walked across the campus.

"I've dreamed I was a poodle," Mookie said. "And then I dreamed my pizza was talking to me. I wasn't a poodle that time. I was a hamster. The pizza was pepperoni. With olives that winked. Hamsters love olives."

"What's so special about this place?" I asked Abigail. I knew it was a famous college, but there were tons of colleges all over the country.

"Everything. Can't you just feel how wonderful it is?" As soon as she said that, I guess she realized I wouldn't even feel anything if one of the buildings fell on me. "Well, you know what I mean."

"I guess." The students I saw walking around the campus didn't look all that different from the ones at Romero Community College. They were just big kids carrying books. Some were wearing fancy clothes, and others were in torn jeans.

We found the gym. There were twelve tables set up for the teams. This time, there wasn't so much of an audience. I spotted people who were obviously parents. Some of them had large signs or banners. I also spotted Mr. Murphy, who was dressed like a college professor. But I was a good enough spy not to wave at him. Or laugh.

I studied the other teams. You can't really tell how

smart people are by looking at them, but sometimes you can get an idea how good they are at athletic stuff. From what I saw, the competition would be tough. There was definitely a lot of muscle in the room. On the other hand, I was pretty sure nobody was going to make us step into a boxing ring.

All of the tables had small signs taped to them. I found ours: BELGOSI UPPER ELEMENTARY, EAST CRAVEN, NJ. There was a name card on the table in front of each of the three chairs. I was in the middle. Happily, there was no sign of a team name.

A guy in a tan corduroy suit greeted us. I noticed his tie had a picture of Shakespeare on it. After we sat, he explained the rules: For the academic part, three teams would compete at a time. It was a little different from what we'd done at Belgosi, since there were more teams. The first round would narrow things down to four teams. Then, all four would compete in the physical part. The two highest scorers would compete in the final creative-thinking part.

"We just need to win one academic round," Abigail said. "That's good. I'll bet there are some real smart kids here. This is Princeton."

"Yeah, we're in Princeton," I said. "But that doesn't mean any of the teams are from here. We're the winners from southern New Jersey, right? That means we're from closer to Princeton than anyone else."

"So one of the teams could be from Harvard, or

Yale." She said those names like they were magical places. "Or Dartmouth or Cornell."

"Abigail, they're all from elementary schools. Just like us."

She ignored me. "I'll bet there's someone from NYU or Columbia. Swarthmore! Rutgers! MIT!"

I had to stop her before she named every college on the East Coast. "Check out the signs. Harker Elementary. Dunwich Academy. Lovecraft Upper Elementary. They're all just kids. They're exactly like us—except not as smart." I gave her a smile, but I could tell she was still nervous.

"Duke!" she said. "Brown!"

Mookie leaned past me and put his hand on her shoulder. "Look, Duke is a dog's name and Brown is just a color. I don't know what a Swarthmore is, but it doesn't sound very tough. And Princeton—that sounds like a prince who weighs too much. You need to forget about all that stuff and just be a smarty-pants show-off. I think I know what will help."

He hunched over and got that look in his eyes.

"Not now!" I said. The last thing we needed was for him to clear the gym with a blast of gas.

"What are you talking about?" He reached down to dig through a pocket in the leg of his pants, pulled out a tiny plastic rabbit, and slid it across the table to Abigail. "I got you this for luck. I couldn't find a rabbit's foot."

"Uh, thanks." Abigail took the rabbit. "I'm not superstitious, you know."

"Neither am I," Mookie said. "But I believe in good luck."

Our team got to go in the first round, which didn't make things any easier for Abigail. The guy in the suit stepped up to the microphone and started the competition. He told us his name was Dr. Phibes. Then he read the first question.

"The topic is geography. Name the longest river in Europe."

There was a pause of at least a second and a half. It seemed like a century. I was used to Abigail answering the questions way before they were finished.

Finally, she reached for the buzzer, but she moved her hand like the button was red hot and she didn't want to touch it.

Buzzzz.

A kid on the Laughton Elementary team said, "The Volga."

"Correct," Dr. Phibes said. That gave Laughton a ten-point lead. Dr. Phibes read the next question. "Who wrote the novel *Animal Farm?*"

The same thing happened. Abigail froze, and Laughton scored. Now, we were down 20 to nothing.

I looked at Mookie. "We're in trouble."

"I have an idea," he whispered.

"Bigger rabbit?" I asked.

"Nope. Not a rabbit. I think Abigail needs to meet a dumb bunny."

I couldn't even begin to guess what he meant by that. But if Mookie had an idea that didn't involve emptying his intestines, that was fine with me.

"Now for a math question," Dr. Phibes said. "The sum of two digits is twelve. Their product is thirty-five. What are the—?"

Buzzz.

Mookie slammed the buzzer and shouted, "Zero!"

"Wrong," Dr. Phibes said.

Laughton got it. We were down minus-10 to 30.

"Next question, on biology," Dr. Phibes said. "In phototropic plants, there is—?"

Buzzzz.

"Vanilla, chocolate, and strawberry!" Mookie shouted.

Everyone in the gym was staring at us. Some of the kids on the other teams were laughing. Abigail turned toward Mookie and opened her mouth like she wanted to scream at him. I could understand her horror. Here we were in what she felt was one of the smartest places in the world, and Mookie was making our team look like total idiots. I had to admit, it was a brilliant idea. He was trying to shock her back into action. I just hoped it worked.

After staring at Mookie for another moment, Dr. Phibes got the correct answer from Harker, then asked the next question. "This one is about foreign languages," the professor said.

I saw Mookie inch his hand toward the buzzer.

"In the small region between France—"

Buzzzz.

Abigail beat him to it. "Basque," she said.

"Correct," the professor said.

Abigail gave me a small smile. "Had to be. Basque is spoken in the region between France and Spain."

"Good thinking. Keep it up."

And that pretty much turned things around. Abigail was back. We killed the other two teams and made it to the second round with a nice score.

I got lucky with the physical section. Two of the three events were for endurance, which I totally rock at. I didn't have to knock anybody out. I don't think that was supposed to be part of the Brainy Brawny competition, anyhow. I'm pretty sure that was just Mr. Lomux's own special way to do things. The third part was strength. Mookie tackled that one, and managed to get third place, which thrilled him.

He pumped his fist in the air as he came back to our table. "The Mookster snags a bronze medal in the intergalactic Olympics."

I slapped him on the back. "Yup—you've dazzled the universe with your powers."

With our score in the first round, and my two wins in the second, we easily made it to the finals.

"Feeling like a smarty again?" I asked Abigail as we got ready for the last round.

"Yeah." She glanced back at the table where we'd nearly lost everything. "I don't know what happened to me."

"You let yourself get impressed by the wrong stuff," I said. "No big deal. Everyone does it."

For the creative round, we had to do a drawing of a horse and make a face out of clay. I'd always been a pretty good artist. Now, when my hand was totally steady, I was even better. I got us an easy win.

"It still feels sort of weird to win anything," I told Abigail after the judges announced the results.

"I know what you mean," she said. "But I think it will be fun getting used to it."

"Regional champions," Dad said as we left the gym. "Imagine that."

"Yeah," I said. "Pretty amazing. I guess we're going to Washington."

That's where the final round would be. The eight regional winners from the United States, along with those from other countries, would all compete in Washington, D.C., two weeks from now. If I could feel a nervous tingle, I'd have been totally tingling. But as always, I was dead calm. And I had to keep in mind that my goal wasn't to win the whole Brainy Brawny competition; my goal was to get RABID to try to recruit me.

That night, right after dark, fireflies swarmed outside

my window. Since it was way too early in the year for them to be real, I knew the lights were a message from BUM. The fireflies formed the word PARK. Then they flew off. I watched them fade into the distance, making scattered bright flashes as some of them exploded or crashed into telephone poles.

Once I was sure my parents were asleep, I slipped out of the house and headed for the park.

14

Ear flicks and flowers

You've done well," Mr. Murphy said. "I couldn't have asked for a better performance. You'll probably draw their attention."

"I have a good team."

"Yes, you do. Now we need to be prepared. There's no way to know how RABID will contact you. Or even when. I suspect the attempt will occur before you go to Washington for the competition. It might not even be obvious. Nobody is going to come up to you and say, 'How would you like to help destroy the free world?'"

"I guess that would be a bad way for them to recruit people." I smiled at the image of someone in a trench coat, with a large hat and dark glasses, slithering up to me and whispering, *Psssst. Want to join the forces of evil?*

"You just have to keep an eye out for anyone who talks to you, or even moves within view. They're going to check you out first. It could be something as simple as offering you two comic books—one funny and one violent—and seeing which one you accept. Or watching your reaction to a staged accident. If you seem like someone they can't use, they won't ask you to meet with them, and our efforts will have been wasted. So you have to make sure to act like an impressionable young man who can be talked into doing bad things."

"I think I can play that role," I said.

Mr. Murphy patted my leg. "I have no doubt. Well, I won't be seeing you again until after you've been contacted."

"Why?"

"We can't take any chances. The first contact could take place anywhere, at any time. The results of the competition will be in the paper tomorrow, and it'll also be posted on the Brainy Brawny website. Baron von Lyssa will know who you are, thanks to your impressive victory score. His people will be watching you, so they can figure out when and where to test you."

"So how will I get in touch with you?" I asked.

"Use the computer game," he said. "I'll be waiting for your message."

Things at school had settled down, just the way Abigail said they would. I guess everyone was getting used to her being smart. And she was getting used to not hiding her brilliance. I think it's like if I suddenly grew six inches taller, everyone would stare at me for a week or two. But then they'd be used to it.

But not everything went smoothly on Monday. I was in the hall on my way to science when Rodney walked up behind me. Just as I caught sight of him out of the corner of my eye, he reached out and flicked my ear with his finger. I was ready. I shouted "Owwww!" and grabbed my ear like I'd been hurt.

But something shot past me and hit the floor. As I pressed my hand against the side of my head, I realized my suspicion was horribly correct.

Rodney had flicked my ear off!

He was staring at me like he wasn't totally sure what he'd just seen. I scanned the floor. My ear was down there, ahead of me, near the wall. I could hear footsteps through it as kids walked by.

I bent over like I was in pain, howled again, and rolled toward the floor, diving between kids who were rushing to class.

Keeping one hand pressed against the side of my head, I scooped up the ear in my other hand. Then, as I rolled farther and turned the side of my head away from

Rodney, I switched hands and pressed my ear back in place. It wouldn't stay without glue, but I could at least let him see a glimpse of it through my fingers. I spread them enough so there was no mistake.

He took a step toward me, staring. Then he pointed a finger at my head. "You're some kind of mutant freak."

"You could get expelled for hitting me," I said.

"It might be worth it." Rodney's eyes narrowed. "I'll catch you later."

I didn't like the sound of that. I really didn't want to be caught. It was bad enough being a zombie. It would be unbearable if everyone in school knew. I ducked into the bathroom and glued my ear back on. My scream of pain echoed against the tiles.

As I turned toward the mirror, I remembered that this was the place where it first hit me that I was dead. Right here in this bathroom, when I'd had the fork in my nose. I hated to think about it, but another truth was hitting me: I was falling apart. Rodney hadn't flicked my ear all that hard. But it flew off. I touched my nose. How long before it fell off? How long before I started to look like something out of a nightmare?

On Tuesday, when I got to school, Abigail told me, "I heard from Uncle Zardo. He's reached the Philippines."

"Great. Did he find the flower?"

"Not yet," Abigail said. "He can only travel around there at night."

"What is he—a vampire?" Mookie asked.

"No. He's had a bit of trouble there in the past," she said.

"He's never going to find the flower," I said.

"Yeah. We need to go there ourselves," Mookie said.

"That wouldn't be a bad idea," Abigail said. "That way, you can drink the cure as soon as it's ready. We should try to get you over there somehow."

"To the Philippines?" I asked. "How am I supposed to do that?"

"You could ask BUM," she said. "They seem to have all sorts of military connections. They could get you anywhere in the world. They jetted you someplace the other day, didn't they?"

I was about to explain to her why that wouldn't work, but I could tell from the way her expression changed that she'd already figured it out.

"They don't want you cured," she said.

"Yeah. If I'm not dead, I can't do useful stuff. I'm just a kid."

"Maybe we can think of some other reason to get them to send you there," Abigail said.

I looked past her. I could almost picture that flower, waiting for me. I wasn't even sure where the Philippines were. If they were far enough away, I guess it wouldn't matter which way I looked.

"Don't worry," Abigail said. "The flower will be there. We can figure it out after the contest. Maybe if you help destroy RABID, that will be enough for BUM."

"I don't think it will ever be enough," I said. "There'll always be more to do. I'll be carrying out missions for them until I rot apart." I couldn't imagine Mr. Murphy ever agreeing to help cure me. Stronger bones were one thing. That just made me a better spy. But if I had a heartbeat and a temperature, if I needed to breathe and eat and sleep, I wouldn't be special anymore—not in the way BUM needed me to be special. I wouldn't be able to travel underwater, sneak past infrared detectors, or hide in vats of spaghetti sauce.

Way back, when Mr. Murphy had first shown me the bone machine, he told me he'd only help me if I agreed to work for BUM. I could still hear his words: *We might strive for the good of the free world, but we're not a charity.*

That reminded me of something I'd wanted to ask Abigail. "Remember when Dr. Cushing called you to tell you the bone machine was working?"

"Of course. What about it?"

"Do you think it might have been ready earlier than that?"

"I never thought about it," Abigail said. "We had a lot of problems to work out. Though, now that you mention it, I thought we'd solved the major issues a month or so before that. But I just figured she wanted to take extra time to make sure everything was perfect."

"I think it was ready sooner than when she called you," I said.

"But Dr. Cushing knew how worried you were about your bones. She wouldn't make you wait," Abigail said.

"Mr. Murphy would," I said. "None of my spy missions needed strong bones. Nothing I did for BUM needed that, not until this Brainy Brawny thing came up."

"So you think he didn't let you have the treatment until BUM needed you to have it?"

"Yeah. I think so. But that's how they work." I wasn't angry with them. Not really angry. Maybe just a little disappointed. But it helped me realize that Mr. Murphy wouldn't do anything for me unless it also helped BUM. If I needed BUM's help getting the flower, I'd have to find some sort of way to trick them. That wouldn't be easy.

15

It's in the Bag

After school, we headed for Abigail's house.

"You know, pretzels are the perfect food," Mookie said. He snapped off half a pretzel rod that he'd pulled from his backpack, shoved it in his mouth, then talked as he chewed. "They're crunchy and salty. And you can dip them in anything. I'm glad I brought extra."

"Most people consider the egg to be the perfect food," Abigail said.

"Ick," Mookie said. "Only when you bake them into cookies."

I didn't join the discussion. It only reminded me that I couldn't eat anything—or at least, I shouldn't. Not cookies. Not eggs. I'd eaten a huge amount of oysters a while ago, but that's one memory I'd rather not hang on to.

As we reached the corner, an old guy staggered toward us, carrying a bag of groceries. He was wearing the sort of hat that old men wear, and a raggedy coat. Right before he reached us, he stumbled. He caught his balance, but the bag tumbled from his hands.

Cans and boxes scattered across the sidewalk. An orange rolled toward the curb.

"Oh, dear!" Abigail stooped down and started gathering the spilled groceries. "Let me help."

"I got it." Mookie chased after the orange. "It's a hard grounder between first and second. The Mookster makes an amazing catch!" He snatched up the orange. Then he grabbed the bag and started filling it back up with the groceries.

I kept walking. Behind me, I heard Abigail ask, "Can we carry it home for you?"

"I'm really good at carrying things," Mookie said. "Except when I drop them. I guess I drop stuff a lot. So don't feel bad. You're in good company. So, can we help you?"

"I'm fine," the man said. "You've done enough."

"Come on, we'll be late," I called over my shoulder. I slowed down and waited for them to catch up.

"Well, that was rude of you," Abigail said when she reached me.

"Yeah, I'd expect that from me, not you," Mookie said. "Wait—if you turn into me, does that mean I'll turn into you, or will I turn into Abigail and she'll turn into me?"

"Why didn't you stop?" Abigail asked.

I shrugged. "He didn't need our help."

"*Need* has nothing to do with it," Abigail said. "This is about helping others. It's about—ohmygosh!" She glanced over her shoulder, then snapped her head back.

"Shhh," I said.

"What?" Mookie asked. "This is another one of those things, right? Something is going on, and I'm the only one who doesn't get it."

I risked a quick glance. The guy was too far away now to hear us. It was safe to talk. "That was one of them," I said.

"Who?" Mookie asked.

"One of Baron von Lyssa's henchmen. He was testing us. RABID wants to recruit people who don't care about others."

"How'd you know it was a test?" Abigail asked.

I opened my mouth to explain, and realized I wasn't really sure. Then I laughed at the answer that came to mind. "I guess you could call it a gut feeling." That was the only kind of feeling I could have these days—even though my gut doesn't feel anything at all.

"That makes sense," Abigail said. "You've been doing

all this spy work. You've gotten lots of training, and gone on different kinds of spy missions. Something about him gave you a clue. Maybe even something you didn't realize you noticed. Whatever it was that tipped you off, the good thing is that you passed the test. They'll get in touch with you now."

"For sure," I said. "As far as they could see, I'm perfect RABID material." That had been close. If I'd done so much as bend down to pick up a can of soup, I would have ruined any chance of destroying RABID. "I guess I should make it as easy as possible for them."

"You mean split up?" Abigail asked.

"Yeah. Now that they know I'm the sort of person they can recruit, and that the two of you aren't, they're going to wait until I'm alone to make contact." I'd learned to think like a spy, and I was pretty sure that's what they'd do.

"Well, I need to go to the library anyhow," Abigail said. "I have a lot of files to scan through."

"I'll help," Mookie said.

Abigail stared at him for a moment, then nodded. "That would be great. I could use the help."

They headed off, and I headed home. When I took off my sneakers, I noticed my toes looked sort of weird. They'd stayed squished together. I pushed them apart, but I realized this was another sign that my whole body was not dealing well with being dead. I needed that cure.

I called Abigail an hour later. That was as long as I could stand waiting. "Any luck?"

"Not yet. I'm hoping they had an exhibit of the an-ima flower somewhere around East Craven or Hurston Lakes," she said.

"It won't be that easy," I said. "Nothing will ever be easy again."

"Hey, we found the Lazarus mullet near here," she said.

That was an ingredient from the first cure. She was right. We'd found it at the local aquarium. That didn't cheer me up. "We were lucky," I said.

"Maybe we'll get lucky again. I'm going to scan through every newspaper in the library until I find some-thing about the anima flower," she said. "They have papers from all over the state. They're all stored on microfilm."

"Microfilm?" I'd never heard of that.

"It's like pictures of each page. Except they're not on a computer. They're on film in spools. You just have to look at the paper one page at a time."

"That could take months." I wasn't even sure if I had weeks.

"I'll do my best," she said.

I heard Mookie shout, "I'll help!"

It made me feel good. But not hopeful. Maybe I needed to start thinking about what I should do if I couldn't get cured.

But I really didn't want to think about that.

o o o

When I got to school the next day, Abigail and Mookie both looked like they'd rubbed hot sand in their eyes.

"We were at the library until it closed," Mookie said. "I must have skimmed through a couple hundred old newspapers."

"Any luck?" I asked.

"Not yet," Abigail said. "But I know the information is there. We'll keep looking until we find it."

"What about Zardo?" I asked.

"He's having a bit of trouble. I got a long message from him yesterday." Abigail reached for her phone. "This is just the start of it."

FLOUNDER SMOG

LACED ROPE

"It's not good, is it?" I asked.

Abigail brought up the translated message:

FLOWER FOUND, SEEMS WRONG

LACKS EXPECTED PROPERTIES

"There's more," she said. "Basically, it looks like the anima flower might not be a cure, after all."

"He's the only person in the universe who makes more mistakes than I do," Mookie said.

"Ohmygosh!" Abigail spun toward Mookie. "Say that again."

Mookie shrugged. "You trying to make me feel bad? Okay. I'll say it again: He's the only person I've met who makes more mistakes than I do."

Abigail reached out, grabbed Mookie's head between her hands, pulled him forward, and kissed him on the forehead. "Genius!" she said.

"Huh?" Mookie staggered back.

"That's it!" Abigail said. "Don't you see?"

Mookie and I both shook our heads. We didn't see.

Abigail pointed at me. "Why are you a zombie?"

"I was splashed with Hurt-Be-Gone," I said.

"Right. But it was supposed to remove bad feelings. It wasn't supposed to stop your heart and lungs and keep you from feeling physical pain."

"Yeah, I know that," I said. "But your uncle used the wrong flower." I froze for an instant as I heard my own words. Then I shouted out Abigail's favorite exclamation. "Ohmygosh!"

"What?" Mookie asked.

"The wrong flower!" Abigail and I both shouted at him.

I put my hands on his shoulders. "You are definitely a genius."

He backed away. "Don't kiss me!'

"Don't worry," I said. "You're safe." I let Abigail finish explaining.

"Think about it—we haven't found any information about the anima flower. The flower he finally found doesn't seem to have the right properties. There's only one explanation that makes sense. Uncle Zardo got the name wrong again. There's a cure out there. I know it. We just have to find the right flower."

"How?" I asked.

"Research. The instant school gets out, I'm off to the library." She turned back to me. "Any contact from RABID?"

"Nope. But I know it will come."

"So you keep waiting and we'll keep looking," Abigail said.

"That sounds like our best plan."

It turned out I didn't have to wait very long.

16

Choose It or Lose It

After all the high-tech ways Mr. Murphy had contacted me, I wasn't ready for RABID's method of sending messages. I was heading home from school early—we had a half day—when a guy walked up to me and held his hand out. He shoved a slip of paper at me. "Here, kid. Take it."

The instant I grabbed the slip of paper, he turned and walked off.

I wanted to shout something at his back, like, *Hey— you call yourself a spy? Come on, use some imagination! That was pathetic. Why don't you just scream at me from across the street and wave a big sign.* It would have been fun to start ranting, but I knew I couldn't do anything that would let them know I wasn't a normal kid.

I looked down at the paper. There was just one sentence: *If you'd like to meet people who think the way you do, and who appreciate your abilities, go to the corner of Adams and Firth at three p.m.*

So that was it. They'd made contact. They'd probably lead me around for a while, like Mr. Murphy did the first time I'd gone to BUM headquarters. Or maybe someone would just show up with a car to take me to meet Baron von Lyssa. Either way, all I had to do was go to that corner, and I'd be on my way to helping destroy RABID. BUM would follow me and capture Baron von Lyssa.

When I got home, I went to the computer and sent a message to Mr. Murphy through the *Vampyre Stalker* game, like I'd done when we'd first met. I kept it short. *Adams and Firth. Three p.m. Today.*

Ten minutes later, Abigail was banging on my door. Mookie was with her. "I have good news, bad news, and good news," she said.

"How come it's never just good news?" I asked.

"I guess that's the way the world works." She held up a photocopy of an old newspaper article. "Anyhow, the good news is that they had a special exhibition of the animus flower at the Nalbazuna Botanical Garden fifty years ago. That's the plant we need. I did the research. It has all the right properties."

"Fifty years ago?" I asked.

"That's part of the bad news," Abigail said. "That was the last time the flower was on display, which explains why it took so long to find an article about it. And the botanical garden closed about thirty years ago."

This wasn't sounding like it would help me. "You said there was other good news?"

"The gardens were closed, but they were never torn down. Everything is still there," Abigail said. "The flower should be blooming now. It's a perennial, so it wouldn't have died out. It will be easy to recognize. It's silver. They say it almost glows. And even if it died, we should still be able to find some seeds, so we can grow it here."

"Silver? Glows?" I thought back to RABID's lab. I realized I'd already had an animus flower in my hand. But I'd destroyed it. I guess that didn't matter. Not if Abigail had found another one.

"Yup—that's how it's described. I think it also might be very sensitive to death. You might not be able to touch the petals. But I can handle it."

I knew she was right about that. "Great. We can get it tomorrow. Or even this evening, right after I meet with Baron von Lyssa. Where is this place?" I'd never heard of it, but I don't pay much attention to stuff like botanical gardens. I knew there was one in Delaware, because Mom dragged Dad there every year for some sort of special exhibit. He always threatened to get her to drag me along instead of him, but I knew he'd never actually be that cruel.

Abigail looked away from me and muttered something that sounded like "Brazil."

"What?"

"Brazil."

"I hope there's a Brazil, New Jersey," I said.

"There might be," Abigail said. "But we need to go to the one in South America."

"Oh, man. Maybe we can figure something out. But it will have to wait until tomorrow."

"It sort of can't wait," Abigail said. "That whole area is about to get flooded. They're damming the river tomorrow."

"Tomorrow! This isn't good news, bad news, good news. You forgot to add about five more *bad news*es at the end."

"I didn't want to make you feel there was no hope. There's lots of hope. But it's now or never." Abigail opened her purse and pointed to a bottle filled with a clear liquid. There was a battery taped to the side of the bottle, with wires running through a cork in the top. "I brought the rest of the formula, so we can add the flower as soon as we pick it."

"Electricity!" Mookie said, pointing at the battery. "I knew that was the answer."

"It's *part* of the answer," Abigail said. "I have to run a low voltage through the liquid until the blossoms are absorbed. Electricity wouldn't help at all without the flower."

Mookie started dancing around and waving his arms in the air. "I was right. I was right. I was right."

Abigail shut her purse and sighed. Mookie kept dancing. I didn't feel like dancing. I looked at the clock in the hallway. It was almost two. I felt like I was being torn in half. Though if I'd actually been torn in half, I wouldn't have felt a thing. "But I can bring down RABID," I said. "I'm supposed to meet them at three."

"Maybe you could put an end to RABID," Abigail said. "You don't know for sure. All sorts of things could go wrong."

"There's no way we can get there in time," I said.

"There's a way," Abigail said. "I've got it all figured out."

"We don't know for sure if the cure will work, either," I said. I looked at Mookie. "What do you think?"

He stopped dancing. "You're asking my advice?"

"Yeah. You've been with me from the start," I said. "I need to know what you think."

"You're in fifth grade," Mookie said. "Save yourself today. You can try to save the world tomorrow. Come on. Abigail is right. We need to get that flower."

"I could save the world. . . ." Everything we learned in school—all the books we read, all the movies we saw, all the legends and myths—the hero always sacrificed himself to help others. That's the way it was supposed to happen.

Abigail put a hand on my arm. "Mookie's right.

You've got your whole life ahead of you to do good things for the rest of the world. You've already done a lot. Do something good for yourself today."

Save the world or save myself?

I knew she was right. "But how are we getting there?"

"You were in the room when Mr. Murphy called in a jet, weren't you?" Abigail asked.

"Yeah. He did it the other day. And I've seen him do it several other times."

"So you just need to log in to the site and get a jet for us," she said.

"But there's a password," I said. "I remember seeing the *x*'s appear on the screen when he typed it."

"So you should also be able to remember which keys his fingers hit when he typed the password," she said.

"No way."

"Try it," she said. "Or we could stand here and watch you rot."

"I'm tired of watching myself rot." I went to the computer and pictured Mr. Murphy ordering a jet. The Web address popped into my mind. I typed it in. There was a log-in screen, just like the one I remembered. I played the scene back, and watched Mr. Murphy's fingers.

"It worked," I said as the site accepted my entry. "I'm in."

"Great," Abigail said. "Now we need a fast jet."

"No problem." I clicked the box for "highest speed."

I couldn't believe I was doing this. And I couldn't believe it would work. But I had no other choice.

Abigail gave me the code for the local municipal landing field. "I have the coordinates for our destination," she said, holding up a sheet of paper. "Come on. Let's get going."

"This is a joke, right?" Mookie said. "You're just doing this to get my hopes up."

"No joke," I said. "You're getting that jet ride."

We headed three blocks south of my house, where we caught a bus that went past the municipal field.

"I knew this was a joke," Mookie said when we got out. "Nobody's here."

I looked at the empty field. A couple of small prop planes were parked in a hangar. There wasn't anything else in sight.

"They'll be here," Abigail said. She pointed east, past the landing strip. "They'll probably come from that direction."

We stood facing the way she'd pointed, waiting. We didn't see a thing. Not even any birds.

And then I noticed a shadow on the ground in front of me. I looked up.

"Whoa . . ." It was high above us, and coming straight down for a landing.

"Yeah, whoa . . . ," Mookie said.

The jet settled down in front of us. It was like the one I'd been in before, but larger. The cockpit opened up.

I walked ahead. "Transport for three." Abigail handed me the slip. I passed it to the pilot. He nodded. If he was surprised to see three kids waiting for him, he didn't show any sign of it.

"We'll need you to wait to bring us back," I added as I climbed into the jet. "It won't take long." I hoped I was right.

17

A River Runs Near It

A wesome?" **I** a**S**ked Mookie after we climbed out of the cockpit.

"We left awesome behind when we shot through the clouds," he said. "That was beyond amazing."

I was glad he'd finally gotten his jet ride.

"It shouldn't be more than a mile or two," Abigail said as we walked away from the landing area. She led us down a trail.

"This is like a jungle," Mookie said.

"This *is* a jungle," Abigail said. "We're not far from the edge of the rain forest. The growth is tamer here, which is lucky for us. And there should be a trail the whole way."

Every once in a while, she checked a map on her phone. "Almost there," she said after we'd been walking for nearly half an hour. "We just have to cross a stream."

We heard the rush and the whirr at the same time. I looked ahead as we broke through into a clearing. We were facing a river. It wasn't really wide, but the water was moving along pretty quickly.

"Stream?" I asked.

"Stupid map." Abigail glared at her phone, then looked at the river. "We'll be okay. It's too fast for us to swim, but those rocks should get us across."

She was right. There were plenty of large rocks we could scramble across. But the whirr was getting louder. I looked over my shoulder.

"Did you ask for a helicopter?" Mookie said.

"Nope." I watched it hover behind us and start to land. There was just one person in it. He was looking toward the hillside across the river.

"I'll bet it's someone from RABID," Abigail said. "They probably want the animus flower so they can do more zombie experiments."

"We have to get there first," I said.

"And we have to keep them from getting there at all," she said.

The helicopter settled down behind us. I guess the hillside was too steep for it to land.

"Come on," Abigail said. "We don't have much time. Let's get across. We'll think up a plan after we reach the other side."

We started to cross the rocks. Some, in the shallow water, were barely large enough to stand on. Others, where the water got deeper toward the middle of the river, were as big as cars.

"I have an idea," I said. "You go ahead. But stay out of sight once you've made it across."

Abigail looked like she was going to ask me about my plan. I held up a hand. "Look, this is spy work. Trust me. I know what to do."

At least I hope I do.

I checked the rock to make sure my plan would work. There was no other rock to step on at this point. Whoever was heading for the other side would have to cross this one. It was also large enough for what I planned, and had slick moss on it that would make the job easier. I slipped into the water and let the current press me against the rock. Once I was sure I wouldn't get carried away, I ducked down below the surface. Now I just had to wait.

It didn't take long. I saw his shadow before I saw him. The second his foot landed on the rock, I popped out of the water, grabbed his ankle, and yanked hard toward the back of the rock.

It worked. He splashed into the water. I clung to the side of the rock and watched as he thrashed his arms. The current swept him downriver.

I got back up on the rock and hurried across.

"Wow," Mookie said. "That was cool."

"Good thinking," Abigail said. "Come on. The building has to be this way. The sooner we get out of here, the better I'll feel." She led us up the hill.

There was a trail, but it was overgrown. The hill was pretty steep. By the time we reached the top of the ridge, I was the only one who wasn't puffing and panting.

"Man, I've got to sit for a minute," Mookie said.

I grabbed his arm and said, "Watch out!"

"What?" Mookie asked.

I pointed to the side of the trail where he'd been about to plunk down. "That's agony vera—it's a cactus full of toxic juices. If you get even a little scratch, you'll itch for weeks."

Abigail stared at me. She was usually the one with the knowledge.

"I read about it when I was testing my memory," I said. "Then I saw it in the lab."

I thought she'd be annoyed, but she just smiled. "I'll have to read up about it. It sounds fascinating."

"It sounds dangerous." Mookie took a careful step away from the edge of the trail. We moved on and pushed through some high shrubs.

And there it was.

"That looks like one of those scenes from those pocket lick movies," Mookie said.

"Pocket lick?" Abigail asked. "What's that supposed to mean?"

"You know," Mookie said. "Those movies where life on Earth gets wiped out by a comet or aliens or something."

"That's *postapocalyptic*," Abigail said. "Not pocket lick."

"Hey, that's too hard to say," Mookie told her. "Besides, *pocket lick* sounds cooler. It's like you're always carrying around something sweet." He jammed his hand in his pocket, then took it out and licked his fingers.

Whatever the word, he was right about the way the place looked. There was a gate in front, but most of the wall had collapsed. I could see some walkways, but they were broken up and overgrown. Nature was taking back the land.

"There are buildings over there," I said. I could see a wooden shack and three larger buildings. They all looked pretty run down.

We reached the shack first. The doors had fallen off. I looked inside. It was some sort of toolshed, with a broken-down lawn mower, rakes, shovels, pruning shears, hedge clippers, and a bunch of other rusty tools.

We walked past it. "Let's try here." Abigail headed for the next building. A sign in front, written in several different languages, read RESEARCH LIBRARY.

"That won't be it," she said. But she glanced in anyhow. Just to make sure, I guess.

The next building was a cafeteria and gift shop. We moved to the last one. The sign read: EXHIBIT HALL.

"That has to be it," Abigail said.

The door had fallen off, and part of the back half of the roof had collapsed. "This doesn't look very safe," I said.

Mookie laughed. "It's not like it will kill you."

"But it could kill you," I said. "Let me check it out first."

Abigail and Mookie agreed that wasn't a bad idea. When I went in, the floor creaked a bit, but it seemed solid enough. There were tables all around with flower-pots on them. Nothing was blooming. To the left, I saw a collapsed staircase, like the ones they put in video games when they want you to find a different way to get to the second floor. The bottom half had fallen apart. The top half drooped at a steep angle. A carpet dangled from the steps like a tongue.

To the right, along a good part of the wall, there was a hole in the floor. I went over and looked down. That area was probably a basement, but it was too dark to tell what was there.

Farther ahead, I saw that part of the second floor had collapsed, too. The wood slanted down to the first floor, like a ramp. At the top of the ramp, in a room that ran along the whole rear wall, was a collapsed table and a large, broken flowerpot. In the dirt that had spilled from the pot, I saw a cluster of flowers. Shimmering silver flowers—just like the ones I'd destroyed on my mission. I had to make sure not to touch the blossoms, or they'd wither.

"Hey," I called toward the door. "I found the flower. It's safe to come in, but watch your step."

They joined me.

"Is that it?" I asked.

"Yeah," Abigail said.

"How do we get up there?" Mookie asked.

"I don't know." We were so close. "Maybe we can climb this." I gave the end of the carpet a tug. A piece tore off in my hands. It was too rotted to hold my weight. The stairs swayed and groaned. There was no way anybody was climbing them.

I went to where the fallen part of the second floor touched the first floor and tried to step up on it.

"Oof!" My foot went right through the wood.

"Let me try. I'm lighter." Abigail managed to go two or three feet before the wood started to splinter under her.

"Careful!" I reached out and grabbed her arm as she toppled back. "This isn't going to work."

"Oh, no!" Abigail pointed at the flowers.

As I watched, one of the petals fell. "How long do we have?" I asked.

Abigail squinted up at the flowers. "An hour or two. Don't worry. The petals won't all fall off at once."

"Hey," Mookie called. He'd moved over to the wall

right next to the hole in the floor. "I found a light switch. Maybe there's a ladder in the basement."

"No!" Abigail said as Mookie flipped the switch.

"What's the big deal?" he asked.

"That's not a light switch. It's for a generator or something," she said. "It's been sitting around for thirty years."

Mookie shrugged. "So it won't work. Which means there's no problem."

Lights flickered in the bulbs on the ceiling. More light flickered from the hole.

"Or it will work just fine," Mookie said.

Whumpffff!

We all looked over toward the hole in the floor.

"Or it will catch fire," Abigail said as smoke drifted from the basement.

18

The flower Bowl

Fire.

I had a lot of bad memories about fires. So did Abigail.

I looked at the floor, then back at the flower. "How long do we have now?"

"Ten minutes," Abigail said. "Maybe less. We need to get some blossoms right now."

I wasted one of those minutes staring at the flower. By then, I knew what I had to do. "Wait outside by the door," I said. "I'll be right back." I didn't want them breathing too much smoke.

I ran out and headed for the toolshed. There wasn't a

ladder inside. I wasn't expecting one, but it would have been nice. And it definitely would have been easier than what I had in mind.

Can I do this?

I thought about when I was trying to get the ingredients for the first cure. I'd broken off my little finger. At the time, it was the hardest thing I'd ever had to do in my life. I guess now I was facing the hardest thing I'd ever have to do in my death. It was a thousand times harder. Partly because of my strengthened bones—mostly because it was just about the most awful thing I could imagine. But I guess I was a thousand times tougher. I'd walked through fire and battled monsters.

I already knew I could find what I needed. I'd seen it when I'd first looked inside the shed. It's a good thing my hands weren't capable of shaking.

Can I do this?

I had to.

But can I?

I did it.

And then, carefully, I walked back to the exhibit hall and joined Abigail and Mookie.

"You're a good bowler, right?" I said to Mookie as he followed me inside. More smoke was drifting from the hole. I could hear the crackle of wood catching fire. We had to hurry.

"Yeah. Really good," he said.

"And you're pretty good at Skee-Ball, too."

"For sure. I can hit those fifties with my eyes closed." He closed his eyes and made a rolling motion.

I looked over at Abigail. She was staring at me like she knew what was coming but couldn't bring herself to believe it. "Are you okay?" I asked her. "You can go outside, away from the fire. Mookie and I can handle this."

"I'm fine," she said. "Do what you need to do."

"Take my head and roll it up to the flower," I told Mookie.

His eyes shot open. "What?"

I pointed at my neck. "I did the hard part. I cut it off. You just have to bowl a perfect throw."

He reached for my head, then froze.

"You can do it," I said. "Aim for the stems."

"What if I mess up?" Mookie said. "I'm always messing up. I'm the one who got you splashed. You're dead because of me. Ever since then, all I've been able to do is come up with crazy ideas that don't help. And now, I'm going to mess you up forever. I'll get your head stuck up there, and you'll never talk to me again."

I was going to tell him to calm down. But that was pointless. I'd never seen anyone calm down just because someone told them to.

"Calm down," Abigail said.

"I'm trying!" Mookie screamed. He blinked his eyes a couple of times. The smoke was starting to bother him.

I knew he'd do it sooner or later. But he had to do it

right now. He might have said he could hit the 50's with his eyes closed, but I definitely needed him to do this with his eyes open. I had a feeling they were about to open wider than they'd ever been before. I reached up and grabbed my hair, then lifted my head and held it out to him.

Come on, Mookie. Don't freeze up now. Smoke was already swirling around our ankles. I saw flickers of flame lighting up the basement.

He reached out and took my head.

It was hard to keep my balance. I saw the world move below me, and then it rose as Mookie lowered my head. He was shaking now. I could tell because everything I saw was vibrating back and forth. I had to find some way to get him to calm down. I didn't have a chance to reach the flower if he stayed this nervous.

Got it!

I knew what to do. "It's the tenth and final frame," I said, trying to sound like a sports announcer who was keeping his voice half-hushed. That was easy, because I didn't seem to be able to talk very loudly right now. I was just happy I could talk at all. I kept going. "The Mookster has already rolled nothing but strikes. This is the very last ball of the game. One more strike, and he's bowled a perfect game."

The vibration slowed from a frantic buzz to a gentle rattle. Good. I just needed to keep his mind distracted. "Not only will this win him the championship, but it will also let the human team defeat the dreaded alien Gargazols who came here to challenge humanity for the universal bowling title. The president has promised the Mookster a lifetime supply of chili-cheese dogs if he can pull off this stunning victory."

Everything moved forward. Mookie took a step. And then another. The world rushed past my face as he swung his arm back. And then I was flying. Spinning and flying. I waved my arms to keep my balance. Then I dropped to my knees. My brain didn't seem to understand that it had left my body. My head rolled across the slanted floor, going up toward the second story. I opened my mouth and got ready to snag one of the flowers. The roll slowed as I moved higher. I could see glowing flashes of silver. I was almost there. If I messed up now . . .

No. Stop that!

I'd been through too much. I'd done too much. I'd fought enemy spies and survived monsters. I could certainly clamp my teeth on a flower. That was easy.

Steady.

One more rotation . . .

Snap!

I shut my jaws, clamping my teeth over the stem of one of the blooming animus flowers. After my experience in the lab, where the flower had withered, I knew I couldn't touch the blossom. Not even with my mouth. But Mookie had made a perfect toss. My head dangled over the edge of the flowerpot.

"Did you get it?" Mookie called.

I almost answered. But I managed to keep my mouth shut. Now I just had to get the flower to Abigail. I used my back teeth to chew at the stem on the side away from the flower. After a moment, the stem broke, and my head fell back to the slanted floor.

It was definitely interesting to watch. I'd rolled down hills before—lots of times. And way back when I was five, I'd fallen down a flight of stairs. But I'd never taken a trip, or seen one, like this.

When I reached the bottom, Mookie snatched me out of the smoke. It was up to our knees now.

"You got it!" Abigail said. She grabbed the flower from my mouth. "Let's get outside. I'll put it into the bottle," she told Mookie. "You glue his head back on."

Oh, boy . . . I'd tried not to think about that part. This was really going to hurt. But if Abigail was right, it would be the last time I would have to feel the pain of the bone glue.

After I stopped screaming, I looked at my watch. It was past five. I'd missed my meeting with RABID.

When we left the exhibit hall, which was nearly filled with smoke now, Abigail held up the bottle. "The flower has to steep in the liquid until it dissolves, and you'll have a cure."

"Once it's ready, will it take long to work?" I asked.

"No. Once it's ready and you swallow it, the effect should be instantaneous," she said.

We passed through the gate. Then I forced my way back through the bushes.

We weren't alone.

As I stepped out, I almost ran right into the guy I'd pushed into the river. He looked wet and angry.

"Hand it over," he said.

He also looked familiar. Actually, double familiar. I'd seen him before—wearing a gas mask in the lab I'd destroyed. I recognized his bald head and beady eyes. But he was also familiar in another way. Not like someone I'd seen—but like someone I'd heard described. I remembered Zardo's words when I'd asked him who had given him the corpse flower.

He was bald with brown eyes. I definitely remember his ears. They were tiny.

He'd also told me the man had an Eastern European or Mediterranean accent. It all matched. This wasn't just the guy who'd grown the corpse flower. He was also the guy who'd killed me. No matter what else had happened, he was the one who brought the corpse flower to Zardo. He was behind all the bad stuff RABID did with plants. I'd destroyed his plants, but it looked like he was trying to replace them. If he could make and cure zombies at will, he could do all sorts of awful things.

"I'm not playing around, little boy. Give it to me right now."

I gave it to him. I grabbed a fistful of my hair with one hand. The glue on my neck wasn't set yet. I remembered the first time I'd glued my thumb back on. I'd moved my hand too soon afterwards, and the thumb had flown off. With a tug, I yanked my head back off my shoulders and thrust it forward. I shoved my head right in his face. At the same time, I opened my mouth, screamed, and stepped toward him. He backed away. Anyone would. Even the bravest person on the planet would have backed up automatically.

And this guy wasn't brave. Bullies rarely are. He staggered away from me, then stumbled backwards and fell right into the patch of agony vera.

His scream was a lot louder than mine. He pushed himself to his feet, which was a mistake since both his hands got filled with the stickers. He fell again—on his stomach this time. I guess he was a slow learner, because he pushed himself back to his feet a second time, getting even more stickers in his hands.

He looked like a porcupine. He spun around like he didn't have a clue what to do, and managed to tumble off the side of the hill. I watched as he rolled all the way down to the river, crashing through lots more agony vera before he plunged into the water. He was still thrashing and screaming as he floated down the river. This time, it didn't look like he'd be swimming back in our direction any time soon.

"He's going to be doing nothing but scratching for the next two or three months," Abigail said.

"I had a dog like that once," Mookie said.

Abigail and Mookie helped glue my head back on. It hurt even worse this time, but it was worth it.

With the cure safely bubbling away in Abigail's purse, we headed back to the jet.

"Let's go home," Abigail said.

I couldn't believe I was just hours away from being cured.

19

Gym Dandy

Normally, I did whatever I could to find ways to pass each sleepless night. Tonight, I just lay in bed and thought about everything that had happened to me since I'd been splashed with Hurt-Be-Gone. I guess I could say my death flashed in front of my eyes. Except, it was more a crawl than a flash.

When I got to school, Abigail rushed up to me. "It's nearly ready." She opened her purse and showed me the bottle. The flower petals were almost gone.

When we got to home base, she peeked into her purse again. "Soon," she whispered.

The loudspeaker crackled. The secretary spoke. "Nathan Abercrombie, please report to the gym."

The gym?

I didn't like the sound of that. I glanced at Mookie. "Maybe you should make a run for it," he said.

That wouldn't work. I would just have to deal with it. The cure would be waiting for me when I got back. I left the classroom and headed toward the gym.

I was halfway down the hall when Rodney turned the corner.

"There you are," he said.

I looked over my shoulder. Eddy was moving up from behind me. "We figured out your secret, freak."

Rodney grabbed my arm. Eddy rushed over and grabbed my other arm. Rodney poked me in the forehead. "It doesn't hurt, does it?"

"Let me go."

They dragged me to the gym. I tried to yank free, but I'd spent so many months watching out for my brittle bones before they'd been hardened that it wasn't easy to force myself to yank my arms. Even if I did, I couldn't break Rodney's grip. I might have strong bones, but I still had zombie muscles.

When we reached the gym, Rodney and Eddy held me against the wall. Mr. Lomux was there, standing next to a cart with a projector on it and a computer. There was a wire running from the computer to a thermometer. I recognized the equipment from science class.

"You think you can walk around with living people?" he asked.

"What are you talking about? I'm just a kid. Let me go." I jerked hard and tried to pull free, but it was no use. I was pinned to the wall like a butterfly in a museum display.

Mr. Lomux walked over to his office and picked up his phone. A moment later, I heard the loudspeaker again. "All students report to the gym."

"You can't do this!" I shouted at him when he came back.

"I can do whatever I want," he said. "And when everyone finds out what sort of monster I've exposed, I'll be a hero."

He turned on the projector. A moment later, I saw a readout of the thermometer on the screen.

"I figured out we could use that," Eddy said. "That was my idea. All mine. I'm still the smartest kid in school. You'll see."

Kids filed in with their teachers. The gym door opened again. Principal Ambrose walked in. "What's going on? Why did you call everyone here?"

"To expose a monster." Eddy pointed at me. "He's a zombie. It all makes sense. We'll prove it."

Mr. Lomux came over to me and held up the ther-mometer. I clamped my mouth shut.

He grabbed my jaw. "Open up!"

I struggled, but I couldn't get away. I was afraid if I fought too hard, he'd tear the flesh right off my face. That would definitely prove his point. There's nothing like a bare jawbone to get the attention of a zombie-hunting mob. Past him, I saw a couple of the teachers start to come toward us. I guess they wanted to stop him. But it would be too late. Once they saw I had no temperature, they'd know I was a zombie. Instead of rushing to help me, they'd run away in horror.

"Wait!"

Abigail burst from the crowd. She raised the bottle. The flower was dissolved now. The cure was ready. But there was no way Abigail could walk up and say she was giving me a zombie cure.

Everyone turned toward her. A couple of weeks ago, they would have ignored her. But the contest had made a difference.

"It's true," she said. "He's a zombie! I've known it all along. I befriended him so I could gain his trust and expose him to the world."

What is she doing?

She walked toward me. "I'll prove it. Step away," she said to Mr. Lomux. "He's more dangerous than you realize. One bite, and you'll be infected, too. We could all get infected."

There was something in her eyes, some sort of craziness that made him obey. He snatched his hand away from my face and moved back. Abigail stepped up to me and raised the bottle.

"My greatest invention," she said. "Zombie tint. It makes the undead turn bright red. How's that for a catchy slogan? Turn the undead bright red." She cackled like a mad scientist and thrust the bottle toward my lips. "There are zombies all around. Maybe even standing right next to you!"

I saw all the kids in the crowd look around nervously.

Abigail kept talking. "Until now, they were safe from detection. They could slink among us and spread their disease. No more. I've saved the planet. I'll be rich!"

She tilted the bottle. I drank the formula.

Please work.

My throat felt warm.

"Behold!" Abigail cried, pointing at me. She stared for a second, frowned, then said, "He's not red. I guess he's not a zombie. Oh, well." She shrugged, turned away, and walked off. But before she turned, she gave me a wink.

My neck and head felt warm.

Mr. Lomux stared at Abigail until she vanished back into the crowd. Then he jabbed the thermometer into my mouth. I didn't resist.

"See for yourself," Mr. Lomux said. "He's a zombie."

I watched the screen. The numbers moved.

"Ignore that," Mr. Lomux said. "The computer's wrong."

Principal Ambrose walked over to me and pulled out the thermometer. He frowned down at it for a moment, then said, "Normal. Unlike everything else that's going on here."

"No! He's not normal. He's dead!" Mr. Lomux screamed. Dozens of veins bulged on his bald head. He looked like he was wearing a gummy worm wig. "Stupid science stuff." He hurled the thermometer against the wall. The glass shattered. "Ouch!" I felt a sharp pain stab at my cheek. Pain. Real pain.

"Watch this!" Rodney flicked my ear.

"Youch!" It hurt, but it stayed on. More pain. I was thrilled.

"Release him at once," the principal said.

Rodney and Eddy let go of my hands. I reached up and touched my cheek, then looked at my fingers. Blood. Not a lot. It was just a scratch. But I was bleeding, just like any normal kid. Just like a living kid. Wonderful, warm, flowing blood. My cheek stung. My ear hurt. I'd never been so happy to feel pain.

"Out!" Principal Ambrose yelled. "All three of you. Lomux—you're fired. I'm calling the school board right now to start the paperwork. And you two—you'll have detention for the rest of the year, after you come back from a week's suspension. Both of you are in a huge amount of trouble."

Mr. Lomux, Rodney, and Eddy slunk out of the gym. Principal Ambrose turned to me. "Are you all right?"

"Yeah. I think so. Thanks."

"Go back to wherever you're supposed to be. All of you." He spun away and walked out of the gym. As the door closed behind him, I heard him mutter. "Let this year end. Please. Just let it end."

"You okay?"

I turned around to see Mookie and Abigail coming toward me.

"I'm good," I said. I held up my hand and wriggled the blood-spotted fingertip. "Flesh and blood. That was an amazing performance, Abigail."

"It was nothing. I just pretended I was Uncle Zardo. Acting is kind of fun." She pulled a tissue from her purse and dabbed at my cheek.

"You did a really good job," I said. "Even I thought you were crazy at first. But it worked. I'm alive."

Alive. Living. Not dead.

The thought made me choke up. Wow. I could feel emotions. I really was alive. I took a deep breath. "That was so brave," I told Abigail. "But everyone is going to think you're totally weird."

"I'm used to that." She touched the corner of my eye, then held up her finger. The tip was wet. "More signs of life." She smiled. So did I.

"So I guess life is back to normal," Abigail said as we walked out of the gym.

"For sure." I punched the door to open it. The wood cracked. "Well, maybe not totally normal."

"What about Mr. Murphy?" Mookie asked.

"I don't know," I said. "And I'm not looking forward to finding out."

20

Spied Out

I figured the summons would come with sparks or lasers. Maybe a swarm of robot ants would crawl up my wall and scorch a message into the paint, telling me where to meet him.

Instead, I saw him on the sidewalk, right outside my house. I'm not even sure why I went to the window. Maybe I just sort of sensed him there. When I looked down, he looked back and pointed around the corner. I slipped out of bed and made my way to the street.

"RABID was waiting for you last night. Everything was in place so we could track you to Baron von Lyssa. And you didn't show up. I was afraid something bad had happened to you," he said. "But you went to school this morning, like you always do." He headed down the street. I followed him.

"Something did happen," I said. "But it was something good."

"Something better than bringing down RABID?"

"For me," I said.

He kept walking. We went two blocks before he spoke again. "Only one thing comes to mind that would fit that description."

"I guess so."

"You found a cure." He didn't say it like it was a question.

"Yeah. I'm alive again. I'm sorry I didn't help bring down RABID."

"So am I."

I didn't say anything.

"There'll be other opportunities," Mr. Murphy said. "I'll bring down RABID someday."

"Are you angry with me?"

"Anger would be pointless. I'm sorry we failed. But I can see how this is good for you. Selfish, but good." He turned and started walking back the way we came.

"Hey, maybe one of the other kids you've found can finish the job." I caught up with him. "What about that?"

He stopped and turned toward me, but didn't say anything. His expression was sort of sad.

Wow. I'd never even thought of it—I guess because

I'd never really been able to think of myself as special. "I'm the only one? . . ."

Mr. Murphy nodded. "So far . . ."

"All those years. That whole organization. I'm the first useful misadventure BUM ever found?"

"Yes. You were it. Come on—it's time to go home."

I realized I'd never see him again. If I went to the Museum of Tile and Grout, the lobby would probably be empty again, like it was the time Mr. Murphy had been kidnapped. There'd be no more training sessions. No more spy missions. That would leave an empty spot in my life.

We reached the corner down the street from my house. Mr. Murphy stopped there.

"So, I guess this is it," I said. As sarcastic as he could be, and as much as he made fun of me, I knew I'd miss him. He'd taught me so much. I'd miss being a spy. I liked going after the bad guys and making the world a better place. "It was nice knowing you. Really."

"What do you mean?" he asked.

I didn't see why he needed me to spell it out. I guess he just wanted to torture me one last time. "I'm no use to BUM anymore. I lost my useful misadventure when I got cured."

"True, you're no use to BUM anymore. But I'm also the head of BETTY."

"BETTY?"

"The Bureau to Exploit Truly Talented Youngsters," he said. "Think of all that you've learned. And all that you've been able to do. Sure, much of it depended on your zombie skills, but you have a quick mind and a brave heart. Don't forget, you've been trained by a master. BETTY can use you."

"Really?" A shiver of excitement rippled from my spine to my gut.

"Really." He patted my shoulder. "Besides, the success of the bone machine has given us lots of ideas for future ways to modify the human body."

"Forget it. I'm not getting anything else changed." I backed away from him. I didn't like the look of enthusiasm in his eyes.

"Think about it, lad. Wouldn't you love superstrong muscles that let you leap over buildings?"

"Nope. The higher you leap, the farther you fall."

"Night-vision? You could see in total darkness."

"Forget it. I like being in the dark."

"Lightning-fast reflexes?"

"Not interested. I might hurt somebody."

"Of course you're interested. Every kid your age dreams about being a superhero. We can talk about it later. We'll be in touch. Keep an eye out for my next message. BETTY has even better technology than BUM."

He turned and walked away.

"Don't burn my house down," I called after him.

"Don't be so tedious," he said. "We've burned down very few houses. But that reminds me—you owe us $87,439.23 for jet fuel. We'll talk about that later."

I guess I shouldn't be surprised he knew about the jet. But I was pretty sure he was kidding about the money. I watched him walk off. Then I climbed back through my bedroom window. I got in bed and pulled up the covers. I was so tired, I figured I'd sleep like a dead person. No, wait. Just the opposite.

For the first time in months, I'd get to sleep like a living person. A real live, normal flesh-and-blood kid. With maybe a couple of superpowers. Not a lot. Just one or two. Or three. Definitely not more than four. Or five.

I closed my eyes and slept.

Later

We went to Washington for the final competition, even though we knew we'd have a tough time. Abigail even wore a Team Mookie T-shirt this time. But she had her mom alter it so it fit better. The trip was a lot of fun, and the Brainy Brawny organizers took us on a tour of the White House. Mookie and I had time to go to the Spy Museum, which was totally cool. We won the academic part, of course, though it wasn't so easy this time. Abigail isn't the only supersmart kid out there. She seemed happy to find other little Einsteins to keep in touch with.

As for the rest of the contest, let's just say we didn't

dazzle the audience. But we took third place, and that's pretty nice. They gave us a trophy for our school.

Now that I was alive, I was worried I wouldn't be able to keep jogging with Dad. But Dr. Scrivello put me on a new asthma medicine, and I can still jog as long as I don't overdo it. I think, if I keep working on my endurance, I might even be able to try out for the cross-country team when I get to middle school.

I'm still doing a bit of spy training. Twice a week, I go to BETTY, which is in the same building as BUM, after school. Mr. Murphy promised he'd have missions for me someday, but he added that there'd be nothing that could get me killed. He laughed for about five minutes after he said that. So did I. I can't help it—I like him.

Abigail has made it cool to be smart. Some of the kids liked her mad-scientist performance—especially the kids who watch a lot of science fiction movies. She's probably the most popular of the three of us. That's fine with me. She's really had the hardest time in life. She deserves a break.

After seeing me pinned to a wall by Eddy and Rodney, most of the kids in school realized I wasn't dangerous or scary. Even Ferdinand isn't scared of me. At least, not more than he's scared of anything else.

Eddy's parents sent him off to a private school, which means Adam is back to being the second smartest kid at Belgosi. Rodney tried to get tough with me after he came back, but I just stared him down. He's left me alone since then.

Mookie is still Mookie. He's the best friend a guy could ask for. Especially a guy who owns a gas mask.

I'm not a zombie anymore. I eat, I breathe, I feel pain. I feel pleasure, too. What can I say? Being half-dead wasn't all bad. But being alive is all good.

ACKNOWLEDGMENTS

Many people helped make this series possible. The folks at Tor Books are at the top of the list. Tom Doherty built a company that builds authors. Kathleen Doherty suggested zombies as a topic way before the rest of the world caught zombie fever. Susan Chang edited multiple versions of each book and somehow remained cheerful under a grueling schedule. Dot Lin and many others helped promote and publicize the book. Without Tor, I'd be dead meat.

Adam McCauley is a genius. His cover art is amazing. My wife, Joelle, helped in countless ways. Were it not for her, I'd be a zombie right now. My daughter, Alison, was always eager to brainstorm. Mark Myers gave me some great suggestions. Dr. Ronald Julia was a great help when I had medical questions. Dave Siegfried of Spring Garden Elementary School was my go-to guy when I needed to check out anything involving elementary schools.

If the title of this fifth book seems familiar, it was in-spired by *Enter the Dragon*. My thanks to Bruce Lee for all he gave to both the movie and the martial arts world. While I'm thanking those I've never met, let me add Tab Benoit, whose CD *Fever for the Bayou* played almost constantly during the time I wrote this series. I should also thank all the legends of horror movies and fiction and all the people connected with zombies or horror in literature, from Ambrose Bierce to Zora Neale Hurston. I had a lot of fun playing with their names in these books. I hope horror fans had a lot of fun hunting out the references.

I owe big thanks to the reviewers, both in magazines and on the Web, who took the time to spread the word, and to the teachers and librarians who know that a book can be both gross and good. It's nice when adults get what I'm doing. I think I need to single out (triple out?) Teri Lesesne, Paul Goat Allen, and Damon Caporaso, among those who appreciated the book on more than one level.

It's impossible for me to name everyone who should be thanked, but equally impossible not to name at least some of them. Special thanks have to go to Rick Kleffel, who gave me my first chance ever to be on NPR, and to the folks at Children's Book World in Haverford, Penn-sylvania, and Blue Marble Books in Fort Thomas, Ken-tucky, who made a special effort to tell their fellow booksellers about this series.

Lastly, I have to thank all my young readers for coming along for the ride. You kids totally rock. And I must say, if you stuck with Nathan through all five books, you have pretty strong stomachs. And pretty cool minds. Thanks.

TURN THE PAGE
FOR A READER'S GUIDE ON

ENTER
THE
ZOMBIE

Nathan Abercrombie,
Accidental Zombie
BOOK FIVE

ABOUT THIS GUIDE: The information, activities, and discussion questions that follow are intended to enhance your reading of *Enter the Zombie*. Please feel free to adapt these materials to suit your needs and interests.

WRITING AND RESEARCH ACTIVITIES

I. Brainy Brawny

A. Nathan's mind is sharp as ever, though his body is falling apart. In the character of Nathan, write a journal entry describing your feelings about this terrible situation. Or, in the character of Abigail, write a letter to Dr. Cushing describing Nathan's condition and explaining how urgent it is that they find a cure.

B. The French philosopher and scientist René Descartes (1596–1650) is famous for the statement *"Cogito ergo sum"* (*I think, therefore I am;* or *I am thinking, therefore I exist*). In the character of Nathan, Abigail, or Mookie, explain what this statement means to you. This can be done as a role-play with friends or classmates, or as a written journal entry.

C. Hold a Brainy Brawny competition in your school or community. With friends or classmates, create a list of competition events. Invite teachers or family members to prepare quiz questions and to invent physical fitness or creativity challenges. Nominate a panel of judges. Create a trophy to award to the winning team.

D. In the character of a RABID spy, record a video message reporting to Baron von Lyssa about Nathan's amazing performance at the Brainy Brawny competition and recommending that he be recruited into your organization. Share your video with friends or classmates.

II. Rotting and Rolling

A. Go to the library or online to find a dictionary definition for the word "rot." Make a list of synonyms for "rot." Incorporate at least five words from your list into a poem or lyrics for a song entitled "I Don't Want to Rot."

B. In the character of Rodney the bully, make a list of observations that lead you to suspect Nathan isn't human. Include these observations in a letter to Mr. Lomax, encouraging him to report Nathan to the principal—or worse (use your imagination)!

C. Go to the library or online to find the meaning of the word "Lyssa." (Hint: It comes from Greek mythology.) Create a short oral report explaining why you think the author chose this name for the head of his criminal spy syndicate. Present your report to friends or classmates.

D. At the end of the story, Nathan removes his own head to save his life. Draw a series of cartoon panels depicting this climactic scene from the viewpoint of Nathan's head or from the perspective of Mookie bowling with this terrifying object.

III. BUM and BETTY

A. You are a government agent assigned to keep the secret file on Mr. Murphy and his organizations BUM and BETTY. Write up a report describing his childhood, education, spy experiences, and how he came to form his agencies.

B. Design a logo or identification card for BUM or BETTY agents to carry. If desired, create a T-shirt, carrying case, or other clothing or gear sporting this logo.

C. Create an application form for kids interested in joining BUM or BETTY. Include a checklist of basic requirements, a list of yes-no questions, and several essay prompts. Make copies of the application for friends or classmates to complete.

D. You've been hired to write the first novel in the next Nathan Abercrombie series, Nathan Abercrombie—Recovering Zombie, in which Nathan goes on a mission for BETTY. Write a short essay or outline describing this story. Be sure to note whether RABID will still be the enemy and what roles Mookie, Abigail, Rodney, and Mr. Murphy will play. Think of a title for your book and, if desired, draw a cover illustration.

1. In chapter 1, Nathan learns about the Brainy Brawny competition, which Mr. Murphy believes is a recruiting front for RABID. Why does this require Mookie and Abigail to become involved? Who are the members of the other Belgosi team enrolled in the competition? What are Nathan and his friends expected to do?

2. Describe some of the ways BUM contacts Nathan and some of the disguises Mr. Murphy wears in the course of the story. Compare this to the way Baron von Lyssa protects his identity and the way RABID contacts Nathan near the novel's end. How does the author use these differences to characterize the two types of spy agencies?

3. In this series, Nathan must deal with or use his zombie status to deal with problems both at school and in the spy world. Compare and contrast these problems in *Enter the Zombie* or other Nathan Abercrombie books you have read. Do you think Nathan learns things from situations with bullies, gym class, and other school issues that help him in the spy world? Is the opposite also true? Share some examples from the novels to support your answer.

4. What partial cure for his zombie status does Nathan receive from Dr. Cushing early in the story? How does this help him? What problems of being a zombie are not addressed by the cure? What is happening to Nathan that makes it clear that there isn't much time left to find a complete cure?

5. What special garment does Mookie create for his Brainy Brawny competition team? In what other ways does Mookie show his amazing enthusiasm for his friends, the competition, or other experiences he has in the novel? Do you think Mookie is an optimist or just a little bit nuts? Do you ever wish you could go through life as happily as Mookie? Why or why not?

6. Describe the Saturday night mission Nathan carries out for BUM in chapters 9 and 10. What zombie qualities are especially useful during this adventure? What does Nathan learn about his destructive powers that is critical to getting the key ingredient for his cure at the end of the story? What does Nathan learn about BUM's access

to expensive government help that is also important near the end of the novel?

7. What accidental comment does Mookie make that helps Abigail understand the final component needed for Nathan's zombie cure? What do Nathan and Abigail come to realize about limits of the help Mr. Murphy and Dr. Cushing will provide? Explain what Mr. Murphy meant when he told Nathan that "We might strive for the good of the free world, but we're not a charity" (page 123).

8. Ultimately, Nathan must make a choice between saving his own life and, possibly, saving the world from RABID. Do you agree with the choice Nathan makes? Why or why not? Would you have made the same choice had you been in Nathan's predicament?

9. At the close of the novel, what do you think Nathan would list as the five best things about being human again? What might he miss about being a zombie? What do you think is the best, most amazing, scariest, or most inspiring thing about being human?

10. In chapter 20, what does Mr. Murphy reveal to Nathan about the other members of BUM? Are you surprised by this fact?

11. After all of the misadventures Nathan has had with BUM, why do you think he chooses to join BETTY? What special qualities or talents will he bring to BETTY? Had you been in Nathan's situation, would you have agreed to join Mr. Murphy and work with BETTY? Why or why not?

12. What has being a zombie taught Nathan about friendship? What has he learned about dealing with bullies? What has he learned about being popular and unpopular? Do you think his experiences as a zombie spy have made Nathan into a better student, son, and human being? Explain your answer.

Read all the
NATHAN ABERCROMBIE,
series by

Paperback • 978-0-7653-1634-9

Paperback • 978-0-7653-2507-5

Nathan Abercrombie is having a really bad day. Things couldn't get any worse…until he gets doused with a potion that turns him into a half-dead zombie!

Nathan jumps at the chance to become the world's first zombie spy when secret organization BUM offers him a cure in exchange for his help. But can Nathan trust them?

STARSCAPE

tor-forge.com/starscape

books in the
ACCIDENTAL ZOMBIE
DAVID LUBAR

Paperback • 978-0-7653-2509-9

Paperback • 978-0-7653-2510-5

When greasy green globs of goop start oozing from every faucet in town, BUM asks Nathan to investigate.

It's a stinky situation when Nathan's school develops a mold problem and he has to find out what's causing it before it pollutes the entire town.

"**Nathan is a delightful hero—a former semi-nerd and frequent subject of smackdowns, adventitiously turned cool customer—which, to zombies, comes naturally.**"
—*Kirkus Reviews* on *My Rotten Life*

If reading about a **ZOMBIE** in your mouth, try

Paperback
978-0-7653-4570-7

"These stories creeped
us out—and we loved it.
Four stars!"

—*Chicago Tribune*

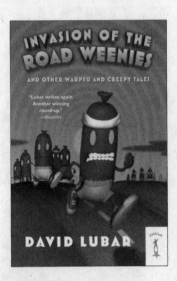

Paperback
978-0-7653-5325-2

"Pleasingly short,
well-crafted pieces...
mixes the comic
and the creepy, the
merely weird with
the truly haunting."

—*San Francisco Chronicle*

And be on the hunt for
Attack of the Vampire Weenies,
available in hardcover in May 2011!

has left a ROTTEN taste
devouring some WEENIES!

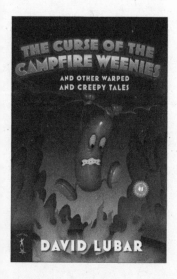

Paperback
978-0-7653-5771-7

Paperback
978-0-7653-6075-5

"This book will talk itself
right off the shelves, and
reluctant readers will
devour it."

—*School Library Journal*

"Lubar's creativity is
still going strong in these
thirty-five short stories...
[that] will delight
reluctant and ravenous
readers alike."

—*Booklist*

tor-forge.com/starscape